ONLY YOU

A MFM MÉNAGE ROMANCE

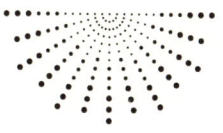

VIVIAN WARD
DEREK MASTERS

ALWAYS BOOKED PUBLISHING

Copyright © 2017 by Vivian Ward & Derek Masters

All rights reserved.

No part of this book may be reproduced in any form or by any electronic or mechanical means, including information storage and retrieval systems, without written permission from the author, except for the use of brief quotations in a book review.

VIVIAN WARD NEWSLETTER

Get free books, ARC opportunities, giveaways, and special offers when you sign up for Vivian's newsletter. We all get enough spam so your information will never be shared, sold or redistributed in any way. You'll instantly receive a free novel just for signing up that isn't available anywhere else!

newsletter.authorvivianward.com

DEREK'S DARK DESIRES

Subscribe to my Dark Desires newsletter and get a FREE copy of Riot instantly! Riot is a full-length novel that is only available to subscribers!

Once you have your free book, you will have the advantage of knowing when I will be releasing my next title, when I'm having special deals, and you'll be the first to know the next time I have some cool stuff to give away (you can unsubscribe at any time).

CLICK HERE TO SUBSCRIBE NOW

For the hopeless romantics, may this book show you true love at it's strongest.

A POEM FROM VIVIAN

Your warm whisper in my ear
    makes my heart grow near.
    I love the way you touch my skin,
    it's hot as fucking sin.
    Please don't stop,
    I love the way you make my pussy sop.
    Hold me close and never let go,
    I promise my love for you will always flow.
    You're the best man on Earth.
    From ashes to ashes and dust to dust,
    I will love you; I must.

CHAPTER ONE

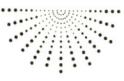

PENNY

Enrolling myself into nursing school is the best thing that I've done for myself since I dumped Owen's ass. I only wish that I would've done it sooner.

Sometimes I think about how stupid I was during our three-year relationship no matter how hard I try not to. To this day, I still can't say exactly what made me stay with him for so long.

Sure, he was good-looking, educated, and polite, but he was also very dull and selfish. Maybe his intelligence is what attracted me to him the most, but I should've known better than to put a man before myself.

I think a lot of younger women do that: put their boyfriend before themselves, and I was no different, but I should've seen the writing on the wall when I put my future on hold for the sake of his.

He didn't have a problem with me quitting school so that only one of us had to work a full-time job—as long as that person was me. Like a lost little lamb who thought she was in love, I quickly obliged because I was head over heels.

My friends and family all told me that he should've been the one working full-time to support us to allow me to go to school, but I naively brushed off their advice and wore a stupid grin plastered on my face all in the name of love.

For three long, tedious, mind-numbing years, I put up with the relationship that we had—if that's what you want to call it, but those days are gone. I already wasted my early 20's, and now that my mid-twenties are approaching, I've thrown out the old Penny and brought in the new.

My first week of school was overwhelming, yet amazing at the same time. It was so nice to sit in class, take notes, learn new things, and meet new people, but now that the weekend is here, I'm ready to unload, so I decide to make a call to my friend, Sabrina, to see what she's up to.

"Hello?" my friend, Sabrina, answers.

"Hey, girl! What are you doing tonight?" I ask her.

"Ugh. I promised to help my sister make centerpieces for all of the tables at her wedding. She's got the whole weekend planned out for us. I'm sure it'll be fun," she says sarcastically.

"Why don't you get out of it and tell her you've got other plans?"

"What other plans? You know me, I never go out," she says.

"You could come out with me, have a few drinks, and have some fun!"

"I wish I could, but I can't. She'll kill me if I don't show up. She's turned into Bridezilla." I can hear her punching the buttons on the microwave. "If I thought she was bitchy before, this wedding has brought out a whole new level of bitchiness."

Sabrina's sister has always been a bitch, which is why the two of them don't get along. I remember when we were teenagers in high school, she used to barge into Sabrina's room any chance she could so that she could butt her nose into our business. Of course, she'd always take any information that she had back to their mom and get us in trouble, so none of us liked her.

"Are you sure you can't get out of it? I'm dying to go out."

"Sorry, Penny, I would if I could, but I can't. Why

don't you call Abby and see if she can go with you? She's usually good for a night out."

"Yeah, I think I might do that. Try not to shove any flowers up your sister's ass," I tease her.

"No promises," the microwave beeps. "Listen, my food's ready, so I'm going to go. Good luck," she says.

"Thanks. I'll talk to you later."

The whole reason why I called her first is because she's more fun to go out with than Abby. Abby's a party girl, for sure, but she also gets fall-down-drunk and usually requires a babysitter all night, which totally kills the mood.

Staring at my phone, I debate whether or not I should give her a call. I don't know what to do because part of me wants someone to go out with, but the other part of me doesn't want to deal with her drunkenness. Before I can make a decision, my phone starts ringing, and it's her.

"Hey Abster," I pick up the phone.

"What's up? Sabrina said you wanted to go out tonight?"

Geez, does she have to blab everything?

"Yeah, I was thinking about going to The Impulse tonight. Are you free?"

I regret the words the instant they leave my lips, but I don't want to be rude. Abby, Sabrina and I have been best friends since our sophomore year of high school. Besides, maybe she won't drink much tonight, or perhaps she will. I know she will, she always does, and she gets in so much trouble when she does, too.

"Not tonight. Sabrina said you wanted to go out, but I have to clean tonight because my parents are coming in the morning. My dad's going to measure my floors to replace them with hardwood, and then he's going to fix my bedroom ceiling fan. We can go tomorrow, though, if you want," she offers.

As much as I'd love to have some company, I really don't want to wait another night, and I don't want to have to babysit her solo.

"Tomorrow night's not good for me," I lie. "I have a lot of homework to do from my classes, and I figured I could use a break before I really dig in, but thanks for the offer."

"All right," she says. "But if you change your mind, let me know. Okay?"

"Will do," I reply.

"I better go. My place is completely trashed, and if I want to get up early enough to let them in tomorrow, I'm going to have to get to bed at a decent time."

"Good night, Abby," I say, hitting the end button.

After a quick shower, I blow dry my hair and find the tightest pair of jeans I own. Owen always hated when I wore tight clothes, which makes me wiggle my ass into them that much faster. Retrieving a low-cut blouse from the closet, I pull it over my head before slipping into a pair of black pumps.

Standing before my bathroom vanity, I put on my gold hoop earrings and begin to perfectly paint my face for the evening. Pulling back my blonde, wavy hair, I apply foundation to even out my skin tone before applying a few shades of eyeshadow. To complete my look, I tightly line my eyes with black eyeliner, brush on a couple of layers of mascara, and, finally, coat my lips in shiny red lipstick.

Owen hated when I wore dark makeup, which makes me smile that much more.

"Good," I say to myself before turning off the light.

Grabbing my purse and keys off the counter, I head out for a night of adventure—at least, I hope. How depressing would it be if I ended up going to the bar alone and sitting by myself the whole time?

I quickly dismiss that thought as soon as I walk out of my apartment complex when a group of guys hanging around the front entrance whistles at me as I walk past them. With my chin tilted high, I smile as I slide into the driver's seat and start the engine.

Tonight will be fun.

"I wouldn't have it any other way," I say, backing out of my space.

CHAPTER TWO

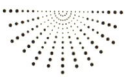

MASON

"Why don't you rack 'em while I grab us a couple of beers?" Lucas says to me.

"Yep, and don't forget, it's my quarter, so I go first."

He mocks me, mumbling under his breath, "It's my quarter, so I go first," as he walks away, bobbing his head from side to side.

I rack the balls on the green felt that's worn down to almost nothing. Everything about this table is original, which is why it's one of the few that are still only a quarter. It has to be at least 25 years old, but it serves its purpose.

"Here," he sets down a tall glass filled with foamy amber-colored liquid.

Taking a swig, I let the ice cold beer quench my thirst

before I set it on the ledge behind the pool table so I can break. I sink the orange five and call solids.

"Come on, Mason," he says after I sink two more balls. "Scratch and give me a turn."

"You don't like it when I run the table?" I laugh at him.

"No, I don't like it when you take my money," he counters.

My winning streak is up when I accidentally sink the eight-ball. "Fuck! You win," I say, knocking back the rest of my beer. "I'll go buy the next round while you rack and break."

"That's more like it," he says.

Flipping him off, I walk over to the bar to buy us another round of beers. The barkeep is cute, but she's not really our type.

Yes, I said our type. Lucas and I share everything.

Everything.

From cars, jobs, friends, and women, we share everything. The only thing we don't share is a bank account.

I summon the bartender by holding a $20 bill up in the air. "Another round of beers for my buddy and me, please?"

She pours two draft beers, and I tell her to keep the change before taking them back to the pool table. Lucas breaks but doesn't sink any balls.

"You're up," he says, taking a drink from his cup. "You know, there's something that makes a beer taste better when someone else buys it."

Rolling my eyes at him, I lean over the pool table to take my shot, and in walks the sexiest woman I've ever seen. Her legs practically go clear up to her neck in her black jeans that look like they're painted onto her round, bubbly ass. She's wearing a low-cut blouse that lays perfectly over her breasts, showing just enough cleavage to leave a little—very little—to the imagination.

Lucas and I look at each other, and we're clearly thinking the same thing. He grins at me and nods toward the same woman.

"Now, that's hot," he says.

"Yeah, she is." I can't take my eyes off of her, she's absolutely gorgeous. "You ever seen her before?"

We come to The Impulse pretty regularly when we're in town, which is often since my family lives here and we do a lot of construction work in the area.

"Nope," he steps next to me. "Can't say that I have, but now that I've laid eyes on her, I'd like to see a lot more of her," he says.

"Make that two of us," I agree with him.

Our pool game comes to a halt as we watch her take a seat at the bar and order a drink. Lucas and I like to observe women before making our first move, so we continue watching her until after the barkeep serves her a pink girly drink.

Resting my chin on the pool stick, I say to Lucas, "Think she's here alone?"

"Maybe. She's awfully dressed up, and I don't see a man with her." He takes the next shot and sinks a striped ball. "Stripes," he calls.

Keeping my eye on the girl, I take note of her long blonde hair and her perfect skin. She's definitely here alone. There's no way any man would let a woman like her go out to the bar by herself.

No fucking way.

"You're up," he says, smacking my leg with his pool stick.

"Ow! You fucker! What was that for?" I rub my leg.

"Gawking and taking too long," he says, leaning against the ledge as he drinks his beer.

He might've given me shit for looking at her, but he's staring, too. As I'm taking my shot, I decide to sink the eight ball on purpose. I want to go talk her before he does and the loser always buys the beer.

"Come on," he says. "What'd you do that for?"

"It was an accident," I shrug. "I'll go grab us another round of beers while you rack and break," I say.

Leaving Lucas standing at the pool table holding his stick, I walk over to the bar and stand next to her. It only takes a second or two before she notices me standing there when she looks up and smiles.

"Hi," she says, her voice soft and smooth.

"Can I buy you a drink?" I ask.

She laughs at me, her cheeks turning slightly rosy as she shakes her head.

"You just cut straight to it, don't you?"

Leaning against the bar, I prop myself up with my elbow as I drink in her beauty. This woman's body screams pure sex, yet she doesn't seem the slutty type.

"My name's Mason," I say, extending my hand. She doesn't take it right away, so I say, "And you are?"

A giggle escapes her perfect lips. "Penny. My name is Penny."

She tries to shake my hand, but that's not why I gave it to her. I grab hold of her hand and pull it to my lips, planting a kiss on the back of her hand. Slowly, she pulls away from me, but I can tell that she's not entirely sure that she wants to.

"It's nice to meet you, Penny. What are you drinking tonight?"

She looks down at her drink and grins. "A cosmopolitan."

"Bartender?" I raise my voice to catch her attention. "Two more drafts and a cosmopolitan for my friend here." She nods and walks away to make the drinks.

"Your friend?" Penny asks. "You're awfully presumptuous."

"Do you like to play pool, Penny?" I nod at Lucas who's watching the two of us like a hawk.

"I suck at pool," she says.

"That's my friend Lucas," I say, nodding toward the pool table. We're both used to this game, so right on queue, he waves at us. "Come play a game with us."

She shakes her head. "Nah, I don't think so."

"Why? Are you here with someone?" I look around. I know she's not; she's just nervous, but we'll get her loosened up—in more ways than one.

"No," she says. "But I already told you, I suck at pool."

"Ahh," I wave my hand, dismissing her excuse. The bartender sets our drinks on the counter, so I pay. "That's no excuse not to have fun. Come on, Penny. Play with us. I bought you a drink, so you owe me," I give her a playful wink.

She draws in a deep breath and sighs. "All right. I'll play, but no making fun of me."

"I wouldn't dream of it," I say, grabbing the beers off the counter. "As a matter of fact, we'll help you."

She follows me over to the pool table where I introduce her to Lucas.

"Nice to meet you," she says. "Now, your friend

Mason invited me to play even though I told him I suck at it, but he promised the two of you will help me."

"Absolutely," Lucas says to her. "You're in good hands here. We'll show you all the moves."

Lucas and I grin at each other as she chalks up the end of her pool stick. She has no clue what kind of hands she's in, but he didn't lie. We are good—at everything. Judging by the look of her body, I'd say she's good at a few things herself.

"So," she says, sweeping her hair away from her face. "Who goes first?"

"Ladies first," Lucas says.

"Yes, ladies first," I agree with him. "Ladies always cum first."

My comment goes over her head, but Lucas gets it, and we both laugh.

"I'm not an idiot, I caught that," she says.

"Well, it's true. When a woman's with us, we always make sure she cums first."

CHAPTER THREE

PENNY

"I suck at breaking," I say. "I can never really break them all up."

"There's a trick to it," Lucas says, walking behind me.

Mason's sitting near the ledge, drinking his beer. I totally caught all of their dirty remarks, but I don't care. I came out for a night of fun, and there's no harm in some playful flirting—especially if it's dirty. Besides, he's cute.

They're both cute, actually. For a minute, I thought maybe they were brothers, but after I came over to the pool table, I can see that they're not.

Lucas is about 5'10" with evergreen eyes and a somewhat pointy chin. His light brown hair is short and spiky, and a little thin, but he's not going bald. It's just thin.

Mason's probably 6'1" with pure hazel eyes, and his

face is more square, but he's very handsome. He's somewhat more masculine than Lucas, but like I said, they're both equally attractive. His dark brown hair is almost black, and it could use a trim, but I like the messy look.

"Here," Lucas says, putting his crotch against my butt as he forces our bodies to lean over the pool table. His solid chest is pressed against my back as he wraps his arms around mine and covers my hands with his, and I'm almost embarrassed to say that I can feel my panties getting a little wet. "When you break," he begins. "You have to aim the cue ball just right, and when you go to strike it," he cups his hand around my arm. "You have to hit it with just enough force."

Pulling my arm back and forth in a slow rhythmic motion, I can't help but think that this is precisely how he likes to be jacked off. Seductively, he places his mouth right next to my ear when he says, "And then you just hit it," his breath moves my hair, tickling my neck.

For the first time ever, I had a clean break, but I didn't sink any balls; though I have a feeling he'd like to sink something right into me as close as we're pressed together. I frown knowing that I didn't do well, but they were right, this is fun.

We just started, and I'm already having a great time with these two. Maybe it's the flirting, perhaps it's the way these two behave when they're together, but they're both so fucking hot. When I turn around, Mason's staring at my ass and doesn't even try to hide it.

"My turn," he says, getting off the barstool.

I sit in his seat and sip my cosmopolitan as I watch him. Lining up his shot, I watch the muscles in his arms flex with every tiny movement he makes. It's hotter than hell, and when he takes his shot, he sinks two balls at once—both solids.

"Now that's how you want to start off," he teases. "Come here, I'll give you some pointers. I'm much better than Lucas."

I bet he is, in more ways than one. Maybe I'm more attracted to him because he came over and talked to me first, or maybe it's because he's the taller of the two, but I'd definitely say that I like him more than Lucas; although, they're both very hot.

Getting out of my seat, I walk over to him where he's waiting for me with a handsome smile on his face. He has a small dimple that I hadn't seen before, and I love it on him. It's very suiting for him.

"Here, take the stick," he says with a slight laughter catching in his throat.

"Very clever," I say.

Doing as he says, I take the pool stick from him, and he wraps himself around my body like a glove, holding me tight as the two of us stretch over the table just as I had with Lucas. My panties are still slightly wet, but with Mason's skin pressed against mine, my nipples begin to tingle.

Taking our shot, I completely miss. The white cue ball slowly spins and bounces into a few balls, but I don't sink anything. Shaking my head over the pool table, Mason sweeps my hair back from my face and whispers, "It's okay. Next time, I'll make sure it goes in."

His warm breath tickles against my skin, and I break out in goosebumps. For a second, I can envision him pushing me over the edge of the pool table, fucking my brains out right here in the middle of the bar. I get the feeling that his friend, Lucas, would probably join in on it, too. Of course, I'm purely basing this on the fact that they're both flirting and coming on to me, yet neither one of them seems bothered or jealous by it.

After a few more drinks and a couple more games of pool, we're all pretty buzzed and having a blast. The three of us have been laughing and touching and drinking for more than a few hours, and being around these two makes me feel sexier than ever. They both make me feel very....wanted.

The bartender yells, "Last call!"

I'm a bit sad that the night's coming to an end, but I guess all things have to at some point.

"Hey, Penny," Mason says. "How would you like to take this party and make it a little more....private."

I look at Lucas to gauge his reaction, and he's all smiles. "Yeah, come home with us," Lucas says.

"Come home with you?" I ask.

That sounds much different than what Mason just said, but I have a feeling they know something that I don't.

"I have a place," Mason begins. "It's not much, just a small two bedroom house, but we can all go there to hang out."

"Do you two live together?" I ask.

It's a legitimate question. They seem like best friends, and I could see them sharing a place. Mason laughs and puts his arm around me.

"Something like that. So, are you in?"

Both of them are eying me, and even though I should probably say no, I nod and say yes before I can stop myself.

"Good, let's get out of here," Lucas says. "You can just follow us."

We walk outside where it's still very warm despite it being almost 1 AM. The summer heat has been awful, and I can't wait for fall to finally get here. This might be the hottest August St. Louis has seen in a long while.

Lucas and Mason climb into a white pick-up truck that reads 'Hunt Construction' on the side. Climbing into my black Toyota Camry, I buckle up and check my makeup in the mirror as they start their engine before we head back to Mason's place.

We've spent the last few hours together having a lot of fun, but I have a feeling things are about to become more interesting.

CHAPTER FOUR

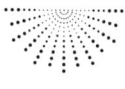

MASON

"You think she'll be game?" Lucas asks on our way back to my place.

Looking in the rearview mirror, I see Penny's little black car trailing behind us. "I think so. She seems a little on the wild side."

"Yeah, she does. Do you think she's ever had a threesome before? It might not be her first time," he comments.

"I don't know. She could also be trying to figure out which one of us likes her." I glance over at Lucas as he shrugs his shoulders. "Penny seems like a smart girl, she'll figure it out soon enough."

"With a body like hers, how could we both not like her?" he laughs. "She's a hot little number, isn't she?"

I nod. "That, she is."

We pull up to my dad's old house. It's one of the very

few things that he owned, and it still feels strange without him here. The house needs quite a few repairs, but since we're mostly on the road for work, I haven't had time to do much to it. If we could stay in town long enough, I could probably have the whole thing renovated in about six months by working on it here and there. There's just not enough hours in the day to get it done sooner.

"So this is your place?" Penny says as I unlock the front door.

"Yep, home sweet home," I say, pushing the door open to allow her to go first.

Hanging my keys on the hook near the front door, Lucas and I follow Penny inside. She seems interested in the house and very curious as she looks around.

"Want a drink?" I ask them as I head into the kitchen.

"Bring me a beer," Lucas yells as he turns on the stereo.

"What do you have?" Penny asks.

Opening the fridge, I look inside. It's a pretty sad sight. There's a carton of eggs, which are half used—and expired, a case of beer, a small tub of butter, some cheese, a pitcher of water, and something hidden under aluminum foil; probably leftovers of some sort. I toss the whole plate in the trash. There's no telling what's underneath the foil.

"We have beer and," I look above the cabinets where I keep the hard liquor, "some vodka."

"I'll take a beer," she says.

Walking back into the living room, Penny and Lucas are standing in front of the stereo talking about music as they decide what to put on. I hand each of them a bottle of beer and admire Penny as she looks through our CD collection.

Lucas excuses himself to the restroom while Penny pops in a CD.

"This is one of my favorite songs," she says, tagging a swig from the bottle.

"What'd you find?"

Before she can answer, the song comes on, and I know what it is just from the intro. She's playing Pony by Ginuwine. Her hips start to sway to the beat of the music, and she starts singing.

"I'm just a bachelor, looking for a partner," she looks me dead in the eyes and points to my chest.

I could definitely be that person for her. Lucas comes out of the bathroom and stands by my side as Penny continues to dance for us.

"Someone who knows how to ride, without even falling off," she points to herself and shakes her hips as she lowers her ass to the ground.

Lucas and I look at each other. We now have the

answer to our question, she's game. Without saying a word, we grin at each other and nod. We're both thinking the same thing.

"Gotta be compatible, take me to my limits," she runs her hands down each of our chests, grabbing the waist of our jeans, pulling on them.

Before she can get another word of the song out, Lucas and I grab her and lift her up in the air. Each of us begins kissing on her neck; she tosses her head back, granting us full access to her throat.

"You sure you want us to take you to your limits?" I ask.

Lucas is busy planting kisses all the down to the front of her cleavage, while I nibble on her ear.

"Ohh," she moans, nodding her head yes. "I'm sure."

"Let's do it," Lucas says.

We carry her to my bedroom because that's where my full-size bed is. There's only a small twin bed in the second bedroom where Lucas sleeps when we're in town. The three of us collapse on top of the mattress, Penny in the center of it all.

Lucas takes her left side as I take her right side. Together, we begin undressing her and ourselves. She's more eager than either of us had anticipated, and it's so fucking sexy to see her practically begging to suck our cocks, but we make her wait.

Her lustful eyes stare at our cocks as she licks her lips. As fun as this is, and will be, we've done this more than a dozen times before, and it's always better when the focus is on her. We get what we need from it regardless, but when the woman enjoys herself, that's what makes it so much hotter.

Pulling her shirt over her head, we each take a breast and free it from the black bra laced with purple trim, exposing her nipples. While Lucas flicks and nibbles the nipple on his side, I lick and suck the other. She's obviously enjoying this, but I can sense that she's nervous. Her body's too tense to be fully relaxed.

"Don't be nervous," I whisper in her ear. "Nothing's going to happen that you don't want to happen, okay?"

Biting her lip, she nods her head but her body doesn't relax, so I decide to help her with that. Lucas is still busy licking and sucking her breasts, so I reach down and begin unzipping her jeans before pulling them down. She's wearing a matching pair of panties that goes with her bra that's now hanging off the edge of the bed. Sliding them down her thighs, I spread her legs and bury my face between them.

She's perfectly shaved and already so fucking wet. Her skin is glistening with her juices. Slowly and deliberately, I lap them up and lick her clean before I sink my tongue into her sweet little hole. She's fucking delicious.

Her body begins to relax as I tongue fuck her and let her come all over my face, but I'm not done yet. I give her a second to recover as I trail kisses along her thighs. Glancing up at her, Lucas is kneeling next to her head. She's sucking his cock, taking him all the way to the base. For a split second, I'm jealous, but then I remember that I'm the one tasting her sweet pussy.

Cupping her ass in my hands, I dive back in, but this time I go straight for her button. Lightly biting it, I pull her clit into my mouth and begin sucking on it. A slight moan fills the room, and her ass starts wiggling in my hands. It's not much longer until she's almost ready to come again.

I back off of her clit and insert my finger deep inside her before going full force again. In two seconds flat, she's coming all over my hands and face once more as her moans fill the room. Her legs quiver as I continue lapping her sweet juices before I let her finish writhing before I climb up next to her, where Lucas and I trade places.

As soon as I'm next to her, she grabs my face and pulls me to her, kissing me as if her last breath depends on it. She greedily tastes herself on my lips as she moans while Lucas tastes her sweet nectar. I watch his head dip between her legs as she tosses her head back.

"Mmm," she says. "I taste so fucking good on you."

"So fucking sweet," I whisper.

Still kissing, I swallow her moan as Lucas brings her to an orgasm. Her back is arched, and those perfect pink nipples of hers are begging for attention. Leaning down, I begin sucking on them as she takes my cock in her mouth.

Swirling her tongue around the head of my cock, she hits every damn nerve ending known to mankind. I lean my head back, trying to concentrate on anything but what she's doing so I don't blow my load.

I've never had a blowjob as good as hers as she teases my cock and sucks it like she's starved.

"Fuck," I moan. If she keeps this up much longer, I'm not sure how long I'm going to last. That's when I decide to switch up the game and make things more interesting.

CHAPTER FIVE

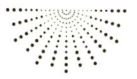

PENNY

"Are you ready to go further?" Mason asks me, pulling his cock from my mouth.

My eyes are watering from taking both of them all the way in my throat. These guys are packing some heat. They're both so big and thick.

"Mhmm," I purr. "I'm ready for whatever you guys want to do."

Mason reaches into his nightstand and pulls out a box of condoms, taking one for himself and passing one to Lucas. My mouth is practically watering as I think about taking both of them. I've never had a threesome before, but I'm ready.

Rolling on his condom, he lies down next to me. "Climb on," he says, grabbing my hips. "We'll let you get comfortable before Lucas joins in."

I've only had anal sex a few times with my ex—not Owen; it was with my boyfriend before him. I just hope this time goes better. Straddling Mason, I slowly take him in. He's much thicker than I thought because it takes a minute for me to fully accommodate his girth.

"You all right?" his deep, throaty voice whispers.

I nod, "Yeah, feels good," I say. And it's true. He feels fantastic and we're only getting started.

His hands keep hold of my hips, and he slowly starts to move them up and down, raising and lowering me onto his cock.

"Mmm," I say. "You feel so good."

"So do you," he smiles up at me. "You good?"

Lucas is behind me, in between Mason's legs, patiently waiting, slowly stroking himself to keep his erection.

"Yeah, I'm ready."

Lucas reaches over to the dresser where there's a bottle of lube sitting on top of it and liberally applies some on himself and on my ass. Massaging my back entrance, he begins to get me ready by sliding his finger in, and it feels so....different.

I've never had both of my holes filled at the same time, but I want more. I want his cock inside me.

"Oh, she's dirty," Lucas says, laughing. "She's ready for more."

"Yeah?" Mason asks, looking at me, waiting for an answer.

"Yeah," I say, still slowly riding his cock. "I'm ready."

Lucas removes his finger as Mason becomes completely still, allowing me to let Lucas enter me. Pressing the head of his cock against my hole, I can feel so much pressure. He's much bigger than my ex who I let fuck me in the ass, and I'm so nervous. I'm afraid it's going to hurt, and my whole body tenses as I embrace for what I imagine is going to be an intense pain.

"It's okay, you're going to be fine," Lucas says, talking me through it. "We'll take our time and give you all the time you need, but I promise, this is going to be amazing. You just let us do all the work."

Mason leans forward and begins sucking on my nipples, making my entire body tingle as he very slowly moves his hips, fucking me from underneath. Lucas squirts a little more lube onto the head of his cock, and before I know it, he slides right in as I focus on Mason and what he's doing to my body.

It doesn't hurt one bit.

"Are you all right?" Mason asks, still moving beneath me.

"Oh god," I say. "It feels incredible."

I can feel my body relaxing as I give in to both of them. Very slowly, Lucas begins moving his hips, pulling out of me and pushing back into me. They each find their own rhythm, moving opposite of each other, and I've never felt anything so damned good.

Mason is moving much faster than Lucas, but I want more. I want both of them fucking me at the same time, using me simultaneously. Thrusting my hips, I force them both deeper inside of me, and for the first time in my life, the sensation is so overwhelming that I can feel myself on the brink of an orgasm from the double penetration.

They can sense it, too. I know they can. Growling, Mason shows his teeth and begins bucking his hips harder, still holding onto my waist. Lucas grabs hold of my shoulders, pulling me back toward him and starts fucking me faster. I try to hold out, but I can't. I've never felt so full in my entire life, and it's sensory overload.

Every single thrust, back and forth, as they work in opposite rhythm makes me shake uncontrollably as I begin to come from my first DP orgasm, and it's fucking amazing. The build up is too much and I finally lose it.

Melting between them, I sink down as I come all over them, but they hold me up, supporting me between the two of them and keep going, delivering thrust after thrust until they each drive themselves to climax and come at the same time.

A slick, sweaty mess, the three of us are intertwined, and I'm completely spent. I've never come so many times or orgasmed so hard in my entire life. I'm not a smoker, but after tonight, I could definitely use a cigarette. The sex was so good. No, scratch that, the sex was fanfuckingtastic!

Lucas pulls out of me first, and then Mason. Lying on top of Mason's chest, I try to focus my eyes, but my vision is blurry from coming so hard. I can still see stars. Pushing my hair away from my face, he gently tucks it behind my ear.

"How was that?" He asks me.

I laugh as I draw in a deep breath, "It was good."

"Good?" his eyebrow shoots up. "That's all? Just good?"

Exhaling a deep breath of air, I say, "If I'm being honest, it was fucking amazing."

"That's more like it," Lucas says as he climbs back on the bed after removing his condom.

Mason pulls his off and tosses it into the trashcan by his bedside. "Was that your first time?"

"My first time?" I laugh. Do these guys really think I'm a virgin? I've never seen a virgin take a double penetration the way I just did, but if I ever saw one, more power to her. "No, I'm not a virgin."

They both laugh with me. "You were pretty fucking tight, but that's not what I meant. Was that your first threesome?"

My cheeks glow with embarrassment, partly because it was silly of me to think they could possibly mean a virgin and partly because it was my first threesome. With the way they performed, they've apparently done this a few times.

"I think it was," Lucas chimes in. "Am I right?"

I'm almost glad that he butted in and said that because I didn't know how to respond to Mason's question.

"Yeah, you're right."

"Ah, so we've got a good girl on our hands," Mason says.

"Yeah, a good girl turned naughty as fuck," Lucas laughs, and it's catchy because we begin to laugh.

"Hey, I've been known to be a dirty girl a time or two," I say in my defense. "Just because I have an innocent face doesn't mean that I am. Looks can be deceiving, you know?"

"We're just messing with you," Lucas slaps my ass. "You're a lot of fun."

"A lot of fun," Mason says. "How many more beers would it take to get you to do it again?"

I can tell he's teasing, but he has a serious look in his eyes. To answer his question, I'd say none because I'd do it again in a heartbeat, but I decide that I probably shouldn't respond with that answer.

"Oh, I don't know. How many would it take you?"

I look at Lucas who's laughing. "It wouldn't take us any. Mason and I share everything. Always."

Turning my attention back to Mason, I study his face, and when he doesn't laugh or say that Lucas is only kidding, I realize that Lucas is telling the truth. They share everything—even girls, and they just shared me. I'm not really sure how I feel about that.

I had trouble figuring out which one of them liked me when we were at the bar, and then I thought that maybe the threesome was happening on the spur of the moment, but now I know that I've been wrong all night. They both like me, and this is a regular occurrence for these two.

"So, how does that work? What if I only like one of you?" I ask.

"Which one of us do you like?" Lucas asks. "Because if you want my opinion, I think you like both of us and can't decide, but that's all right; you don't have to."

He's completely right. I have no idea which one I like because I think they're both equally attractive and I hardly know either of them.

"Give her a break," Mason says. "Let's just have fun. Do you want another beer?" he asks.

My mouth is dry, probably from moaning so much and I am thirsty from all the sex. "Sure," I say. "Let me just grab my clothes."

Getting out of bed, the two of them watch me get dressed like it's the most normal thing for anyone to ever do. Suddenly, I feel a bit self-conscious about my body, so I quickly pull on my blouse and my jeans.

"I'm just going to freshen up a bit," I say, excusing myself to the bathroom as they climb out of bed and throw on their boxers.

When I get in the bathroom, I realize that I look like a raccoon. My eye makeup is completely smudged, and my lipstick is gone. Smoothing my hair with my fingers, I try to ease down the crazy patches that are poking out before I fix my makeup.

I'm really curious about their situation or arrangement. I know that they both fuck the same girls, but do they date the same girls? Like, a real relationship? Or do they not do relationships?

Not that I'm necessarily ready for one, but I would like to know. They're both so damn hot. I don't even know if I'm ready for a relationship with school starting back up and just getting out of the horrible relationship that I had with Owen. The thought of his name makes me cringe, especially when I compare the sex we had with the sex that I just had with Mason and Lucas.

It's something I could totally get used to, addicted to even. Yes, it was that good.

CHAPTER SIX

MASON

While Penny's in the bathroom, we slip our clothes back on and head into the living room after grabbing a few beers from the fridge.

We've had a lot of threesomes before, but Penny was, by far, my favorite. She's so much different than the other girls, and I think Lucas senses it, too.

Taking a seat on the couch, we prop our feet up on the coffee table and kick back with our drinks.

"She's a lot of fun," Lucas says.

Pulling the bottle from my lips, I nod in agreement. "Mhm, yes, she is."

"I could get used to her being around," he says.

"Me too, but I don't think she'll stick around, not with

the way we travel for work. She'll get tired of that real fast."

Lucas sighs, he knows I'm right. Girls never stick around because we're always on the road traveling for work. It's not really fair to expect them to hang around waiting for us, though. They've got lives of their own, and we get it.

"Oh, thank you," Penny says, walking into the living room as she picks up the extra beer. "What were you guys talking about?"

Taking a pull of beer from the bottle, her sparkling sky blue eyes stare into mine. They look like a topaz gemstone; they're as gorgeous as she is.

"We were just talking about work," Lucas says.

"Oh yeah? I saw that your truck said Hunt Construction. Is that where you work?"

"Actually, we co-own it. Lucas's father founded it and handed it down to him, but we run it together."

"Oh," she says. "So your name is Lucas Hunt?"

"The one and only," he says. "We probably should've exchanged names a little earlier, huh?"

The three of us burst into laughter. It's pretty typical for us to hook up with random women, but, for some reason, I want to know more about Penny.

"And I'm Mason Rogers," I add to the conversation. "What's your name, Penny?"

She covers her eyes, pretending she's shy, but she's not the shy type at all. Shy girls don't go home with men they hardly know and have threesomes with them.

"Cooper. My name's Penny Cooper. I can't believe tonight. Crazy, right?" she tags another swig of beer.

"It could be crazy every night," Lucas says, winking at her. "We really like you, Penny Cooper."

She giggles. "You know I've heard of your construction company, but I don't think I've ever seen the truck around here."

"That's because it's been around a long time, but after my dad handed it over to me and passed away, we started bidding jobs all over Missouri, Illinois, and parts of Kansas."

Her smile fades as the realization hits her that we travel a lot for work. "So you guys are hardly around?" she asks.

"We come through from time to time, but for the most part, we're not here much."

We finish drinking in silence, and then Penny stands up. "Well, I guess I'd better get going. It's late, and I've got a lot to do tomorrow."

I get up from the couch, "Let me walk you out to your car."

Lucas stays put, playing on his phone.

"Sure, that'd be good," she says.

Walking her out to her car, I decide to ask her for her phone number before she leaves. Most of the women we bring home are just one or two-time thing, and I definitely want to see her again.

"I had a good time tonight," I say.

"Me too, and just so you know, I was telling the truth. I've never done anything like it before."

For some reason, she feels the need to convince me like I need to believe her, which I do, but I don't really care if she has or not.

"I believe you," I say to her, tucking my hands in my pockets. "Listen, before you go, do you think maybe we could exchange numbers?"

She smiles and says, "Sure, I'd like that."

Pulling my cell phone out of my pocket, I ask her for her number and punch it in before sending her a text. Her phone dings and she pulls it out to check the message and starts laughing.

"Really?" she asks. "Just making sure this is your real number?"

We both get a good laugh out of the message that I sent her. "I'm just teasing you. Drive careful, okay?"

"Okay," she says, kissing my cheek. "Have a good night."

Standing in the street, I watch her drive away until her tail lights are no longer visible.

The time we've spent with Penny has been incredible. We were wrong about her all along. Not only has she stuck around, but the three of us have also been having a blast.

Coming home last night was rough after the three-day job that we just finished, but I'm glad to be back. Waking up, Penny's the first thing on my mind. My morning wood is evidence of the dreams that I had about her all night.

It's hard not to think about her since we see each other so much when the two of us are home, and she and I text and talk on the phone almost all of the time while we're working a job away from home. It's been nice having her around. Lucas and I can't get enough of her.

The smell of coffee brewing is enough to drag me out of bed, so I head out to the kitchen to pour myself a cup. Lucas is sitting at my small kitchen table reading The Riverfront Times.

"Anything good?" I ask, pulling up a chair opposite of him.

"Not really. I was looking for some good concerts tonight that were half decent, but all they have is Just Mister, and they suck balls."

Just Mister. I laugh to myself. They're a local St. Louis cover band and he's right, they totally suck balls.

They play a lot of 80s hair band songs, and it's awful. The lead singer sounds more washed up than Alice Cooper. I have no clue how they book any venues.

Sipping my coffee, I think about Penny some more. Last night was incredible, and I want to see her again. I want us to see her again.

"This might sound crazy," I say.

"Probably is," Lucas cuts me off.

"What if we just hung out here tonight? We could run to the liquor store and get some goods."

"And do what? Sit around here staring into each other's eyes like some weirdos or some shit? Don't you want to go out, pick up a hot chic or two? Have some fun?"

I take a long sip from my mug and lean back in the chair. Apparently, Penny hasn't had the same effect on him, but I don't see how that's possible.

"I was thinking that we could invite Penny over again. You know, maybe continue the fun from last night?" I arch my eyebrow at him.

"What? How are we going to do that?"

"I got her number and—,"

"Wait," he holds up his hand, cutting me off. "You got her number? When did you do that? Did you even have time to do that?"

"Yes," I snap. "I got her phone number when I walked her out to her car. It's legit, too."

"Aw shit, Mason's got a crush on someone," he laughs.

I'd try to hide it but the shit eating grin on my face gives me away. We've been best friends for too damn long, and he knows me well.

"Maybe. Think about it," I say to him. "I'm going to go to the nursing home to visit my old man. You coming?"

Ever since Lucas's dad passed away, he likes coming with me when I go visit my dad. I feel like shit that I'm living in his house while he's stuck in a nursing home, but there's no way that I can take care of him on my own. We travel too much for work. As much as I'd like to bring him back home where he belongs, it would mean that I'd have to quit my job to take care of him and that wouldn't do either of us any good.

He nods. "Let me take a shower first. We'll stop and pick him up a sandwich from Subway."

Dad loves it when we bring him sandwiches. It's way better than the slop they serve him where he's at. For that reason alone, I take him food every chance I get.

While Lucas is in the shower, I shoot Penny a quick text and scrounge up some clean clothes to wear today. Laundry has never been one of my favorite things to do, so I let it pile into small mountains before I wash it all.

Mason: Hey, I was wondering if you'd like to hang out at our place tonight.

Within a half hour, I jump in the shower after Lucas, and we head off to see my dad.

"Hey pops!" I say, walking into his room. Glancing over at us, he nods as we approach his bed. "We brought you a sandwich. Are you hungry? We can grab your wheelchair and take you down to the lunchroom."

He takes the sandwich from me and nods his head. His speech is slurred from the strokes he's had, but if I listen carefully, I can usually understand what he's saying, but he still doesn't like to talk much.

Last year, he had a massive stroke that paralyzed the left side of his body and affected his speech. Not only does he slur his words, but he also gets them jumbled up. The doctor diagnosed him with Alzheimer's and dementia shortly after his last bad stroke, which only makes it that much harder to form thoughts and put them into words. He spends a lot of days frustrated and quiet, and it kills me inside.

Lucas grabs his wheelchair while I put his slippers on him before we wheel him down to the lunch room. It's pretty empty. Another family is visiting one of their relatives, playing a board game, and a few staff who are hanging around, setting up for lunch.

Dad slowly unwraps his sandwich with his right hand, but he has trouble because he's left-handed, so I help him.

"How are you feeling today, dad?" I ask.

His hand trembles as he brings his sandwich up to his mouth for a bite. "Like shit," he mutters.

Lucas and I look at each other. We both know he hates it here, but there's nothing I can do about it.

"Are you sick?" Lucas asks him.

"No, I-I want to go home," he insists. "They t-t-treat me like a ch-ch-child here."

"I know, dad. We'll figure something out," I say.

I hate lying to him, but I don't want him to lose hope, either. I've done quite a bit of research, and I've learned that around 50-60% of nursing home residents die within the first year. I don't want my dad to become one of those statistics.

He eats the rest of his sandwich, listening to Lucas and I talk about job bids and different projects that we're currently working on. We've only got the weekend off, and then we have to go work on a job site for the next two weeks in Springfield, Illinois.

Once dad's finished with his food, we take him back to his room where we watch TV with him for a while. There's a show on where a family just brought home a new baby. Dad's grinning from ear to ear, he's always loved babies.

Using his right hand, he points to the TV and says, "Grandbaby. Soon?"

His eyes are filled with hope, and I don't have it in me to tell him no. I'd love nothing more than to give him a grandchild before he passes, but I don't see how that'd be possible unless I knocked up a random woman, which isn't going to happen.

"Yeah, dad, soon," I say, squeezing his hand.

After a while, he drifts off to sleep, so Lucas and I creep out of his room, careful not to wake him.

CHAPTER SEVEN

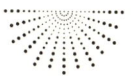

PENNY

I woke up with a slight hangover this morning, but I couldn't let it keep me down. I popped a couple of aspirin, poured myself a big glass of water, put on my headphones, and got started on my school work.

It still feels weird to know that I'm finally going to become a nurse. I've always dreamed of it since I was in the third grade, and now it's starting to become a reality.

All afternoon, I've been engrossed in psychology and anatomy and physiology while jamming out to some of my favorite tunes. You know, all the good ones like Papa Roach, Staind, Shinedown, Godsmack, Bush, Nickelback, Goo Goo Dolls, Matchbox Twenty, and all the other great hits.

Unfortunately, I had to repeat a few of the pre-requisites because I lost some of my credits when I took time off school for dumb ass Owen, but it doesn't matter because nothing's going to hold me back.

When I applied for my student loans, I almost didn't get approved but my mom came to the rescue and co-signed on them. I'm not going to let her, or myself, down.

My eyeballs are burning from studying and taking notes, but my stomach grumbling is what ultimately makes me decide to take a break for some food. Popping some Hot Pockets into the microwave, I grab my phone to see if I have any messages, and I do! I have two of them, in fact.

One is from Sabrina, asking me to please save her from her evil sister who's torturing her with wedding stuff, and the other is from Mason.

Mason: Hey, I was wondering if you'd like to hang out at our place tonight.

Smiling, I decide whether or not I should reply. I want to, but I don't know if I should. Last night was such a blast, but the two of them together kind of blew my mind. Never in a million years did I think I'd ever have a threesome, but damn if it wasn't fun.

Wondering what they're up to today, I take my food out of the microwave and head over to the couch so I can stretch out because sitting at my desk hunched over books all day has my back aching.

I'm about half way finished with my lunch when I decide to respond to him.

Penny: What did you have in mind?

Before I can finish my next bite, his response comes through; of course, I'm all smiles.

Mason: Nothing special. I thought maybe we'd just hang out, have a few drinks, maybe watch a movie or two.

I look over at my desk and stare at all of the books. There are *so many* books, but I've gotten over half of my work done for the weekend. Surely, I can take a night off and finish up tomorrow. It'd probably do me some good so I don't go blind staring at all the fine print.

Penny: Sure, that sounds good. What time did you have in mind?

Mason: How about 8?

Penny: Sounds good. I'll see you guys then.

After stuffing my face with the rest of my Hot Pockets, I wipe my hands on a napkin and bury myself in text books until it's time for me to take a shower.

I'm not sure what I should wear tonight. He said hangout, but what does that mean? Do I wear something revealing and slutty, or should I wear something more homey, like jeans and a t-shirt?

Last night when I met them, I was dressed kind of slutty with heavy makeup, I don't want to show up looking like Susie Homemaker, but I also don't want to show up looking like a high-paid call girl who's ready for another threesome; although, I'm not opposed to another threesome. It was so damn hot last night. I might be in my mid-twenties, but I can still call myself a college girl since I am technically enrolled. You only live once, right?

Getting out the shower, I walk over to my closet and start sorting through clothes. I have so many that it's insane. Picking through my wardrobe, I finally decide on a pair of skinny jeans and a red form-fitting blouse. It's not too low cut, and it makes my boobs look good.

Wiping the steam from the bathroom mirror, I begin blowdrying my hair so I can straighten it and start applying my makeup. I don't want to put as much on as I did last night, but I don't want to look like a plain Jane either, so I put on a liberal amount.

All evening, I've been giddy and excited that Mason texted me, but now that I'm driving over to their house, I'm starting to get anxious. My palms are sweaty and I keep checking my makeup in the mirror as I drive even though I know it looks fine.

Mason and Lucas are sitting on the stairs of the front porch waiting for me when I pull up. Seeing those two together gets my adrenaline going. Before I get out of the car, I wipe my palms on my jeans and nervously tuck my hair behind my ears.

The two of them stand to greet me.

"Good to see you again," Lucas says.

"Thanks, it's good to see you guys again, too."

We all stand on the steps for a minute, waiting for the next person to speak until Mason finally breaks the silence and says, "Let's go inside and grab another beer."

Mason leaves Lucas and me in the living room while he scores some beer from the fridge.

"What'd you do today?" Lucas asks.

"Studied my ass off, took a lot of notes, and started on one of my papers."

Mason returns with our drinks and catches the tail end of our conversation.

"What are you writing a paper on?" He asks.

Neither one of them look like the school type. They're probably asking to be polite, so I spare them all of the boring details.

"It's for my psychology class; it's nothing big," I say, twisting the cap off my bottle.

"Psychology, huh?" Mason asks, taking a swig of beer. "You hear that?" he turns to Lucas. "Beauty AND brains."

My cheeks heat up as I slightly blush. I'm not used to compliments, but they're nice to hear, especially from someone as hot as Mason.

Lucas nods his head in agreement. "Yeah, I'd have to

agree with you there." He holds up his bottle and the two of them clink them together before drinking to it.

"What are you going to school for?" Mason asks.

"Nursing. I just started the nursing program and am working on my LPN before I bridge over for my RN, but I lost some of my credits and have to take a few extra classes this semester."

Mason seems to take great interest in the fact that I'm going to school to become a nurse, and I have to admit, it surprises me quite a bit. The two of us start chatting about my classes, what type of nurse I want to be—which I still haven't decided—and how long it'll take me to finish school.

Lucas is totally put off by the whole conversation and pretty much ignores us while he plays on his phone, avoiding us entirely. After a bit, he stands up and shoves his phone in his pocket as he reaches for his keys on the glass coffee table.

"Where are you going?" Mason asks.

"Huh? Oh, I'm going to meet up with some people. There's a concert in The Loop. I'll catch you guys later."

Mason holds up his beer, "Have a good time. Don't do anything I wouldn't do."

"See you guys later," he says, shutting the door on his way out.

"Did we piss him off?" I ask.

I kind of get the feeling that maybe he's pissed that Mason and I were getting too friendly. They share everything, and maybe he didn't like us talking while leaving him out.

"Nah," Mason says. "He's been dying to go out all day. We work our asses off all week so when we have down time, he likes to have fun instead of sitting around the house."

The truth in his words makes me blink twice. What if I'm keeping him here and he wants to go out? Maybe coming over tonight wasn't such a good idea.

"I can go if you want. I didn't mean to keep you guys," I offer, picking up my phone and purse.

"What? No," he says, pulling me back onto the couch with him. "You're not keeping me at all. I want to get to know you better. Besides, I'm the one who invited you over, remember?"

Smiling, I plop down next to him and put everything back on the table. "So, what do you want to do?"

He grabs my hand and kisses the back of it, "Oh, I could think of a few things, but right now, I just want to hang out with you."

We look into each other's eyes and I've never seen eyes as sexy and caring as his. He leans in and presses his lips against mine.

CHAPTER EIGHT

MASON

Penny is the most sophisticated woman I've ever met. She has such a good head on her shoulders, and she's so smart. How she's single is beyond me, but I'm glad that she is.

There's something special about her, maybe it's the fact that she is intelligent, she has ambitions and goals, and she wants more out of life.

Breaking away from our kiss, I instantly regret the second my lips leave hers and go back for more. I could kiss her all day and spend every night with her in bed.

Pulling her on top of me, she opens her legs, straddling me. Our hands are everywhere; my chest, her back, her breasts, and our lips are crashing into each other over and over again.

My cock is stifled by the zipper of my jeans, begging to be free.

This might sound stupid, but it's been ages since I've made out with a woman and it's hotter than when I was a damn teenager. Back then, I didn't know what to do with a woman but the tide has turned, and I know exactly what to do with Penny.

Flipping her over on the couch, I get on top of her for a brief second before standing to the side and scooping her up in my arms. She squeals and giggles, begging me not to drop her, but I wouldn't do that in a million years. I'm too strong. Working in construction for almost a decade has helped me acquire quite a bit of muscle.

Lying her on the bed, I watch her wavy blonde locks fan across the pillow as she works on unbuttoning her pants, but I don't give her time to take off her pants. I grab the waist of them and yank them down, peeling them off of her in a matter of seconds.

Exposed in her pretty pink panties, I push them to the side and immediately go down on her. Lucas and I share a lot of things, but tonight, she's all mine, and I'm going to savor her sweet taste as long as I can.

Grabbing hold of my hair, she pulls on it as I tease her clit, sucking, licking, and nibbling on it. Wiggling away from me, I pull her back to me. I'm not going to let her get away this easy, not for a second.

Tongue fucking her, I reach up and cup her breasts, squeezing them in the palm of my hands. She has the most amazing tits I've ever seen. They're so full and perfect, and not fake. I've never been a fan of fake boobs. I want them real and soft, and movable.

"Oh, fuck," she whispers, attempting to close her legs as she squirms away from me.

Smiling, I can feel her thighs tightening around my head as her clit swells in my mouth. Increasing the pressure, I flick her clit with my tongue faster and harder, pushing my finger deeper inside her as I curl it to hit her G-spot.

Her hands clench the bedsheets, gripping them for dear life as her back arches and her thighs clamp shut against my head, threatening to squeeze my brain out of my ears while she moans. Coming on my face, I continue a steady rhythm as I feel her swollen clit throbbing from her orgasm, pulsing with each wave that washes over her.

When she can't take it any longer, I ease up the pressure and slowly join her at the top of the bed.

"Come here," she says, turning toward me as she pulls my head to her for a kiss. "I want to taste myself on you."

Fuck! She's so fucking hot. I've never had a girl ask to taste herself on me, but I eagerly allow her to do so because no one should be this greedy with a flavor like hers.

Kissing passionately, my hands roam her body, stripping her of all of her clothes while she removes mine in return. Our bodies are pressed against each other as we cling to one another, both needy and my cock begging to be inside of her again.

She breaks our kiss and pulls her hair away from her face, using her fist as a ponytail as she leans over and puts my cock in her mouth. Her warm, soft mouth takes in my entire length, sliding my tip past her tonsils and down her throat. Covetously sucking my cock, I can feel the muscles in her throat working my shaft. It's nothing like anything I've ever felt before, and I want to come, but I do everything I cannot to so that I don't waste the opportunity to be inside of her.

My hands guide her head up and down as she takes gasps of air, ravenously working my cock. I think about everything: hockey, football, wrestling, anything but how amazing her mouth feels. With a loud pop, she pulls my cock out of her mouth, long strands of saliva and spit still connected to my cock when I grab her and pull her on top of me.

"Come here," I growl. "I need to be inside of you."

Reaching between her thighs, she grabs my manhood and slowly starts rubbing the tip against her clit, teasing both of us. It's insanely ridiculous how good she is at teasing me, and it makes me want her that much more.

"I didn't say anything last night," she says, pulling her hair back from her face once again. "But I'm on birth control. You don't have to wear a condom unless you want to. I'm completely clean."

Lucas and I always wear condoms when we hook up with random women because there's too much shit out there that's easy to catch, but I believe her when she says she's clean.

Putting my hand over hers, I move my cock and line it up with her entrance. "Are you sure?" I ask, applying a bit of pressure to her. Two of us can play this teasing game.

"Oh, my god, yes!" she cries out, allowing herself to sink down on top of me.

She feels so much better without the condom. Being inside of her bareback is hotter than it has any right to be. Raising my hips off the mattress, I push myself deeper inside of her until I bottom out. I can feel her tightness stretched around my cock, and that's when the both of us start fucking so hard that the bed frame feels like it could snap at any moment, but neither of us gives a damn.

When I can't take it any longer, I flip her onto her side and wrap her legs around me, fucking her from the side so I can get in deeper and get better leverage. Within minutes, we're both moaning and grunting as we climax together.

After we've both reached our peaks, she collapses

against me. Both a sweaty mess, we lie tangled together, and I kiss her again as I stroke her damp hair away from her face.

"That was so good," she says, still panting for air.

"Because it was with you," I say, finally sliding out of her.

Looking down between her legs, I can see the mixture of our cum. I'm completely leaking out of her; there's so much cum.

"Here," I hand her a t-shirt, the closest thing to us, so she can clean up a bit.

We lie in bed together, with her in my arms, as we just listen to the sound of cars passing by periodically.

"I love this house," she says. "It has so much original charm and beauty."

Looking around the house, all I see is an old city house, built around 1900. It has tall wooden doors with years of scuff marks that have skeleton key door handles, transom windows above the doorways for airflow, and most of the walls need to be redone.

"It's original all right," I say, rubbing my chin. "I've thought about renovating it, but I don't know."

"Don't know what?" She asks, rolling onto her stomach.

Propping her chin on top of her folded hands, she looks up at me. Her big sky blue eyes look like that of a baby doll. As beautiful as she is, she could be a model. Her olive complexion and blond hair don't match her eyes, but it's a gorgeous combination.

"I don't know if I should remodel the house or not," I smile down at her, looking into her gorgeous eyes. They're such a contrast to her hair and skin. "Do you wear contacts or are your eyes really that blue?"

"Contacts, and don't try to change the subject," she giggles, clasping my hand in hers. "Why don't you know if you should remodel the house? I bet it'd look fantastic with a little work." She glances around the room. "Okay, a lot of work, but you do construction, right? You should know how to do most of it—if not all of it—yourself."

Sighing, I kiss her forehead. "I know, but it's a time thing. Plus, if dad gets out of the nursing home, I don't know what he'd think coming back home to a house that doesn't look familiar to him."

She blinks, "Your dad's in a nursing home? I didn't know that."

Nodding my head, I say, "He's been in there for about four months. He hates it there, but there's nothing I can do. His strokes crippled him, and he requires a lot of care. I'd practically have to quit my job to take care of him full time, and I can't do that."

Lying back on the pillows, she stares at the ceiling with me. "What if you got a different job? Maybe where you didn't travel so much? Surely, there have to be jobs around here that you could work at and make a decent wage."

"Maybe, but I don't know. It's a big responsibility. What if something happened to him and I didn't know what to do? And who would take care of him while I'm at work all day? There are too many what-ifs, you know?"

I've played out different scenarios in my head, but none of them would ever work. Sometimes things are what they are, and you can't change them no matter how much you'd like to.

CHAPTER NINE

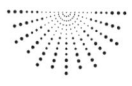

PENNY

I didn't realize that Mason has so much on his plate. When we first met at the bar, I thought that he and Lucas were a couple of carefree bachelors, but I see that isn't the case at all.

"What's Lucas's story? Does he have parents? What's his life like?"

"Lucas?" he laughs. "He's as wild as they come. His dad owned the construction company and passed away, and he never really knew his mom. She was in an accident when he was a boy; I think he was about nine-years-old, so he never really got to know her very well and doesn't have many memories of her."

"His dad left him the construction company?" I ask.

"Handed it over to him, actually. We started running it together, and since he doesn't really have anything to tie him down, he decided to expand the business and take it on the road."

"But you still have your dad? Why would you go with him?"

I get that they're best friends, but I don't understand why Mason would leave his dad behind.

"Without boring you, Lucas needed help, and at the time, my dad was fine. He was retired, doing his own thing. I figured it'd be good for me to learn a trade, so I jumped at the opportunity. He's grown the business quite a bit. We only travel to a few states, but he gets calls for job bids all over the country."

"Why doesn't he take them?" I ask.

Mason sighs, obviously annoyed by my questions, but I want to know the answers. I want to understand where they're both coming from.

"Because I like to come home as often as possible to see my dad. I know what the statistics are for life expectancy in nursing homes. If you're a nursing student, you should know that it's not good."

"To be fair, I've only just started school, but I've heard what you're saying is true. I'm sorry if I'm prying, but I like you and wanted to know more about you."

He wraps his arm around me, pulling me to his chest which is solid muscle—probably from working in construction.

"You're not prying, sometimes it's hard to talk about."

We lie there like that for a bit, just wrapped in each other's arms in silence.

"You know," I say. "If you're up for it, I could go with you to visit your dad sometime."

"You want to visit my dad? Why?" He asks.

"I don't know, just to say hi and see what he's like. You don't have to take me, though."

He laughs, "I'll take you tomorrow. Hell, it might make him happy to see me with a girl for once. I've never introduced him to anyone that I was....," his voice trails off.

"Seeing?" I ask.

"Yeah, seeing," he smiles at me. "You have a way with words, don't you?"

"Sometimes," I bite my lip.

I want to ask him what we're doing or what he'd like from our relationship, but I'm afraid that he'll say nothing. He'll say he doesn't want an actual dating relationship because he doesn't seem like the type of guy to date girls, especially if he's never introduced anyone to his dad.

But I do feel somewhat honored that he's willing to let me meet his dad and introduce me as....his friend? I don't know what he'll introduce me as, but I'm glad that he's taking me.

"You want a beer?" He asks. "I've still got some cold ones in the fridge that we haven't drunk yet."

"Sure," I say, scooting out of the bed with his sheet wrapped around me as I begin to gather my clothes.

"Here," he tosses me a t-shirt and a pair of sweatpants. "You can throw these on so you're more comfortable if you want."

I glance at the t-shirt and frown.

He rolls his eyes. "It's clean, it's not the same one that you used earlier. I did a load of laundry before you came over, so it's safe," he laughs at me.

Smiling, I say, "Okay," and slip on his baggy t-shirt and very loose sweatpants.

Pulling the drawstring tight, I secure them around my waist and follow him into the kitchen. We're about halfway through a movie when Lucas busts in the house, laughing and stumbling with a girl dangling from his arm. By the looks of her, she seems just as plastered as him.

"Hey!" he says, making his way over to the sofa. "This is Brittany. She's gonna crash here tonight."

Before Mason can respond, the two of them are playing tonsil hockey in the living room while Lucas holds her in an upright position because I doubt she can stand on her own.

"Do you need some help with her?" Mason offers, seeing that they're both completely wasted.

"Nah, brother, you handle your business, and I'll handle mine," he slaps the girl on her ass. "We'll catch you guys in the morning."

The two of them stumble into Lucas's room and slam the door. I'm not entirely sure what to make of the situation, but Mason acts as though this is normal.

"Does he always get that trashed when he goes out?" I whisper to Mason.

"Sometimes he doesn't come home because he passes out where ever he goes."

"Is he going to be okay? Are they going to be okay?" I ask.

"Yeah, they'll be fine. Let's watch the movie," he says, turning it back on. "And you can crash here tonight, too, if you want."

Smiling, I snuggle up to him and end up falling asleep on the couch.

The sun is beaming through the sheer curtains hanging on the window. I must've been exhausted because I slept like a rock. Glancing around the room, I realize that I'm no longer on the couch; I'm in Mason's bed, but he's nowhere to be found.

Walking out of the bedroom, I can hear him in the kitchen, shuffling things around.

"Good morning," he says. "Did I wake you?"

He's holding a brown paper bag filled with groceries. I shake my head no.

"No, I just woke up. What are you doing? Do you need some help?"

"You have a seat. I'll make us some coffee. While you were sleeping, I ran down to the corner store and picked up a few things. I bought some eggs. Do you like eggs? I can't really cook worth a shit, but I thought you'd be hungry."

Laughing, I roll my eyes.

"Move," I say, pushing him away from the stove. "You start the coffee, I'll start the eggs. How do you like them? Scrambled, over easy, or sunny side up?"

"You can do all of that?" he asks.

"Of course, I can. How do you want them?"

"I want the yolk runny so I can soak it up with my bread. Can you make them like that?"

I laugh. "Yes, I can make them like that. Should we ask Lucas and his friend if they'd like to eat?"

He stuffs a carton of milk inside the fridge and closes the door. "No, if he's hungry, he can ask whatever-her-name-is to cook for him. We'll have a nice breakfast with just the two of us."

"Okay," I say. "I'd like that."

After I make our eggs and some toast, we sit together at his small kitchen table. Looking around the kitchen, I can tell that it's in dire need of a remodel. It doesn't look like the original wallpaper, but I'd bet it's dated back to the 60s or 70s. It has an awful, faded floral pattern and is stained yellow.

"I was thinking," he says, swallowing a mouthful of food. "Maybe after breakfast, we can go see my dad before we have to head out of town tonight for work? I like to take him something to eat when I can because the food there is terrible. Do you still want to go?"

I nod, "Sure, I can do that. What time are you guys leaving tonight?"

"I thought maybe we could go see him around noon and stay for a couple of hours. We have to start heading out around 5:00 so we can get to the hotel where we're staying and get settled in. We have to be at the job site at 6 in the morning on Monday."

Glancing down at my borrowed clothes, I think about how I need to get ready before we go see his dad. I don't want him seeing me looking like a bum.

"That's fine, but I want to run home to shower and put on something nicer before we go."

He smiles at me. "But you look so cute in my clothes."

"I look like a reincarnated rag," I counter, laughing at myself.

"I'll tell you what," he says. "We'll go over to your place, you can show me where you live, and once you're ready, we'll go see my dad."

It never dawned on me that neither Mason nor Lucas knows where I live. Shrugging my shoulders, I agree.

"Okay, but I'm going to warn you up front: I take a long time to get ready, so be prepared to wait for a bit."

Grinning, he says, "That's fine. It'll give me more time to check out your place."

CHAPTER TEN

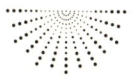

MASON

"I'll try to make it quick," Penny says after giving me a quick tour of her apartment.

It's a cute little place and reflects her personality. There are lots of earth tones with splotches of bright colors mixed in to give it a warm, comfortable feeling.

These apartments were built about six years ago. The workmanship on them is complete shit. They pretty much slapped everything together, which is pretty much what they're doing these days when they build things. Nothing is built of quality anymore. It's like every company is out to make a buck and throw buildings together in a hurry; it's the complete opposite of what Lucas and I do.

We take our time and do things right. There is no cutting corners or taking shortcuts. Our prices reflect that, though, and it's probably why Hunt Construction does so well. Lucas's dad instilled the value of doing things right when he taught him everything he knew; not many construction crews have that quality.

"No problem, I'll just hang out while you get ready."

The sweet scent of her body wash fills the apartment as I walk around stealing glimpses of pictures and look at her things. She's very organized; it doesn't surprise me that she's going to school to become a nurse. There are numerous pictures plastered on her walls and on her desk of her with her friends and family. Books line several shelves suspended on her wall; various romance novels, medical books, and classics such as Stephen King and George Orwell.

A small bookshelf near her television is lined with DVDs and CDs. There are a ton of horror and romance movies; they must be her favorites because they closely match the books on her bookshelves. Thumbing through the jewel cases, I get a sample of her taste in music. It's such an eclectic taste: modern rock, classic rock, some rap, jazz, and a little rhythm and blues. How can one listen to Eminem and Miles Davis?

"Just have to do my hair," she calls from the bathroom.

Tempted to get a peek at her, I crane my neck, but all I can see is the steam rolling out of the bathroom.

"What are you doing?" She yells over the sound of her blowdryer.

Walking to her bathroom, I push the cracked door open and speak up over the loudness. She's wrapped in a thick, white bath towel which hugs her body perfectly. In all my life when I was asked what I wanted to be when I grew up, I never thought I'd say a bath towel, but after seeing her in one, I'm strongly considering reincarnating myself. "I was checking out your place."

She turns the hairdryer off and smiles. "Find anything interesting?"

"You mean besides your love for horror and romance books, or your eclectic taste in music?" I cock an eyebrow.

Grabbing her makeup brush, she begins to sweep powder onto her face. "What kind of music do you like?" she asks. "And don't you read?"

I laugh. "Mostly rock, and no, I've never been much of a reader."

Pulling out her mascara, she begins to coat her lashes. "What? How can you not read books?"

I shrug and push my hands in my pockets to keep from grabbing her and throwing her on the bed. Her cleavage is practically speaking to me with every arm movement she makes, and it's very distracting.

"I hardly ever have time. Lucas and I work so much,

and when we're not working, we like to spend our time relaxing."

She frowns at me as she lines her lips with a tiny pencil. "Reading is relaxing. There's nothing better than crawling into bed with a good book and reading it until your arms get so tired and you're falling asleep that it smacks you in the face."

I can tell by her serious expression that this is actually a thing, and a vision of a book popping her in the nose flashes through my mind, causing me to laugh. "I'd love to see that," I tease.

Rolling her eyes at me, she picks up her flat iron and begins doing her hair. "You wouldn't laugh when it gave you a black eye."

The steam coming off her hair makes me wonder how the hell she's not cinching it off. That thing's got to be burning the hell out of her hair. "Tell me about your music. You have such a wide variety."

She shrugs her shoulders, spritzing some spray onto her hair before she runs her fingers through it. "I listen to different things when I'm in different moods. What's your go-to music when you're sad or angry or happy?"

"I guess it depends," I say, propping myself against the door frame. "When I'm sad, I like to listen to The Fray, but if I'm pissed, I turn on Papa Roach, and when I'm happy, my choices vary. What about you?"

"I have something for everything," she winks at me. "Let me go throw on some clothes and then we can get going."

I turn the corners of my lips down in disapproval. "I like your towel better."

"I'm sure you do," she says, yanking the towel off of her as she walks over to her closet, giving me the perfect view of her ass.

"Such a tease," I moan as she disappears into her closet.

Moments later, she returns wearing a pair of black yoga pants and a loose blouse. It's simple but sophisticated and stunning. She could wear paper towels and look amazing.

On our way to the nursing home, I stop to pick up some food for dad. Since I took him a sub sandwich yesterday, I opt for a pasta bowl from Fazoli's because it's another one of his favorites.

"You know, it's really sweet of you to look after your dad like you do," Penny says as we approach the entrance of the nursing home.

"I've only got one dad," I say, pulling open the door for her. "And we only live one life; might as well make the best of it while we're here this short time on earth."

Nodding, she ducks inside and waits for me to lead the way to his room. As we make our way through the building, I wonder about her parents. She's not said much about them, which makes me question what her family is like.

"Hey, dad," I say, doing my best to sound chipper. "How are you doing today?"

He briefly looks over at me, turning his glance back to the television before looking at me again. Seeing Penny by my side, he raises his good hand and points to her.

"W-who, w-who's this?" he asks.

"Hi, I'm Penny," she says, extending her hand to shake his. "I'm Mason's friend, and he's told me a lot about you."

Dad slowly takes her hand and shakes it, nodding with a smile on his face. "P-p-p," he stutters.

"Yes, my name is Penny," she smiles.

He shakes his head no. "No! P-p-pretty."

She giggles and withdraws her hand from his. "Oh, thank you." She looks up at me and says, "I can definitely see where Mason gets his good looks from."

"Penny, this is my dad, Bill," I introduce them.

"It's nice to meet you, Bill," she says.

Dad can't take his eyes off of her. I'm not sure if he's shocked that I brought a girl with me or if he's admiring her beauty as much as I do.

"Here dad," I hold out the food. "I brought you a pasta bowl. Do you want to go to the dining area?"

Penny helps me get him into his wheelchair, and we

take him to eat. The three of us make small talk, and I explain to dad that Lucas and I will be on the road for a while so I might not make it back for a few weeks. I hate breaking the news to him, but I also don't want him thinking that I abandoned him.

"And as soon as we get back, I'll come visit you just like I always do. Okay?"

His eyes look sad. I know it breaks his heart to be here because it breaks mine, too. When I think about my dad, I still picture him young and strong; invincible. Seeing him weak and fragile is something I never thought would happen, and I know he hates being like this.

Turning his head, he stares outside. "Y-y-yeah," he replies.

We sit in silence for a few minutes until Penny chimes in. "Maybe I could come by and visit while you're away." She turns to my dad, "Would you like if I stopped by to see you, Bill?"

Dad nods his head in approval, making us grin. "Then it's settled," she says. "I'll stop by and see you when I can. Is there anything you like to do? Play cards? Puzzles? Anything?"

I want to stop her from saying anymore because dad gets so frustrated that he can't use his good arm, but his smile stops me dead in my tracks.

"Y-yes," he says. "P-p-puzzle."

"Great! I'll bring a puzzle and some glue. We'll do one together, okay?"

From that moment on until the time we leave, my dad never stopped smiling. When we get out to the parking lot, I stop Penny and ask her why she offered those things to my dad.

"It's good for him," she says. "Mental stimulation is good for everyone, but especially someone in his condition."

"Why?" I ask.

"He clearly displays signs of Alzheimer's, and I'd imagine he may have a bit of dementia. Cognitive brain function is imperative to combat mental illnesses like his. It can help slow the progression of the disease."

Stunned, I don't know what to say. I never told her about his conditions.

"How did you know he has Alzheimer's and dementia? I never told you that."

"It's common for patients like him," she says matter-of-factly.

"And you don't mind spending your time in the nursing home with him? You don't have to do that," I say.

"Not at all, Mason. I'll gladly visit your father. He seemed so happy when you showed up with me, and I could tell that it upset him to think nobody would visit for weeks."

We get in my car and pull onto the main road.

"You've never told me much about your parents, Penny. Where are they? What are they like?"

Glancing over at her, I can tell that I've struck a nerve with her and begin to wonder if I should've kept my questions to myself.

CHAPTER ELEVEN

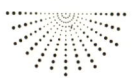

PENNY

I hate when people ask about my parents. Sure, it's common for a lot of people to come from a broken home, but my home was never broken. For something to be broken, it needed to be whole at some point, which is far from what you'd call my family.

Typically, I try to avoid the topic at all costs, but it always comes up sooner or later.

"My mom and I are somewhat close," I say. "She's not the cookie-baking, Christmas-decorating kind of mom, but she's always tried her best. We don't always see eye to eye, and we tend to have disagreements, but I guess that's normal for most people with their parents."

He studies me before carefully asking, "And what about your dad?"

Sighing, this is the part that I most often hate talking

about. I shake my head, "There's not much to tell. I never really knew him. From what I do know about him from my mom, it's best that he wasn't part of my life."

"Wow," he says in disbelief. "I can't imagine my dad not being in my life. He taught me so much and means the world to me."

I can tell how much his dad means to him by the way the two of them interact with each other. It's obvious they've always had a very close bond. Unlike him, I decline the opportunity to ask about the rest of his family. Sometimes, things are best left unsaid.

His dad seemed genuinely happy to meet me. I feel bad that his dad's in a place like that and wish there was something that I could do to improve the situation, but I probably shouldn't get in too deep. We are just 'friends' after all, and maybe it's enough that I've offered to visit him occasionally while Mason is out of town. In fact, I may be overstepping my boundaries as a 'friend,' but his dad seemed to love the idea.

I have another burning question that I'm dying to ask Mason, but I'm afraid to know the answer. The night that I met the two of them, they said that they share everything —which I know firsthand—but how do they do relationships? Or maybe they don't do them at all? Maybe that's why they're both single, but Mason's been growing on me pretty fast and I'd like to be more than 'friends.'

My fear is that he'll say it's part of their unspoken guy code that neither of them can stake claim to me since I was shared by the two of them. I guess it could be kind of awkward to date Mason knowing that I slept with him and his best friend.

I guess I'm more like my mom than I realize. During my entire life, she played partner roulette; she always brought home different men. The ones who stuck around for a while were never the good guys. Honestly, I don't think she ever dated any good ones. My whole life, I've struggled to find out what it takes to make a relationship work, which is why I settled for Owen.

For some reason, I assumed boring equaled good, but it gets old fast. Like my mom, I've always lived life in the fast lane, so I could only handle so much watching TV all the time or sitting around doing nothing, which was Owen's idea of how to spend weekends.

"That's really great that you and your dad were so close. I can see how much he means to you."

He swings by my place to drop me off before heading home to get his things packed. It sucks that he's going to be gone for a while, but I know he'll be back.

"You can call me anytime," he says. "I really appreciate you stopping by to check on my dad while we're gone and hanging out with him."

I smile at him. "It's no problem. Have fun working and be careful driving."

"Hey," he says, grabbing my arm as I try to open the door. "Can't forget this."

Leaning over into my seat, he kisses me. Not a deep, passionate, romantic kiss. Just a regular kiss, a sweet one, on the lips.

My smile turns into a full-blown clown smile that I can't wipe off of my face. "Thanks," I say. "I'll call you."

Over the course of the past couple of weeks, I've stopped by the nursing home to see his dad a few times. Each time was so nice. He was so happy to see me. His eyes would light up, his smile would soften, and his spirit wasn't so....broken. I can see why Mason visits him as often as he can. It really does make a difference in his dad's demeanor.

The first day that I went, we watched a little TV, and I took him some fast food. He ate it, but I could tell that he was bored with his food. After a while, we played a game of checkers, which I let him win, and then I went home.

Last night when I went to visit him, I took him something that Mason could never give him: a home-cooked meal. Before my classes started in the morning, I pulled out my crockpot—which I rarely use because I eat alone most nights—and put on a roast with potatoes and carrots. Before I went to see him, I stopped by my apartment and made us each a plate.

He was flabbergasted to see his meal when I took it to him. I've genuinely never seen a man smile so much and be so appreciative. He chowed down and didn't stop until it was all gone. After we finished eating together, I broke out a puzzle. It was nothing special, just an image of a cabin in the woods with fishing poles sitting at the edge of a nearby lake. He had a little trouble putting it together, but we finished most of it before I left. I promised him that we could finish it at my next visit and I'd bring some puzzle glue so we could hang it up.

I'd go see him again tonight to finish up the puzzle, but I have a lot of studying to do and notes to catch up on. Just as I'm sitting down with my giant cup of Joe, my phone starts vibrating on my desk. It's Mason.

"Hey, you!" I answer. "How's work been?"

"Good. How's school been?"

"Meh, it's school. Professors lecturing, scribbling down notes at lightning speed, studying my ass off, all that jazz."

"I got your text last night about dad. I was going to call you, but by the time we got in, I was exhausted and ended up crashing early."

I laugh at the thought of him being so tired that he crashed because he seems so full of energy. "That's okay. What have you guys been up to all week anyway? Besides working?"

I can hear him getting inside their work truck as he slams the door and I hear the dinging of the key in the ignition.

"Working, drinking, and crashing, that's about it. There's not much else to do on the road," he says.

I'm tempted to ask him if they've picked up any new ladies while they've been out since that's how we met, but I'm afraid to know the answer, so I don't ask. I really like Mason. Like a lot. I like Lucas, too, but I feel this special connection with Mason. It could be because we've spent more alone time together.

"I miss you," I say. The words slip out of my mouth before I can stop them. I'm not entirely sure what made me mention it in the first place.

"You do? That's a first. I don't think I've ever had a girl miss me."

"Well, I do. Where are you guys headed now?" I ask.

"Lucas and I are headed out for a drink before we call it a night."

"Hi Penny," I hear Lucas yell in the background.

Hearing his voice makes me smile. "Tell Lucas I said hi."

I can hear him relay my message and then Lucas says, "What? You don't miss me? Penny, I'm hurt. I thought we had a thing."

Giggling, I say, "Yes, I miss him, too."

"What are your plans for the weekend?" Mason asks.

I think about it for a moment because I hadn't thought about the weekend at all. My mind has been so focused on my studies that I've practically buried myself in notes and books.

"I'm not sure. I'll probably hang out around my apartment, do some studying, and some reading."

He laughs, "You and your books."

"I know. I'll probably go see your dad, too. We have a puzzle to finish, and I'm sure he's eager to get it done."

"Hey, listen. We're at the bar, and it's pretty loud in there. I'll talk to you later?"

"Okay, sounds good. Have fun, but not too much fun."

"Sweet dreams, babe," he says, ending the call.

My heart flutters a little. He's never called me babe. Smiling, I slip on my headphones and crack open my book. I have trouble concentrating on my studies because all I can think about is him calling me babe. He shouldn't have this kind of effect on me, but he does. I also slightly wonder what Lucas thinks of him calling me babe. It's such an odd arrangement the two of them have.

CHAPTER TWELVE

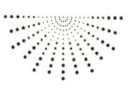

MASON

The last few weeks have been pure hell. This job has really taken its toll on me, and I'm ready to get back home so I can relax and visit my dad.

I'm grateful that Penny has done all that she has. It's nice to know that my dad's been enjoying her company. She gives me updates every time she goes to see him, and it makes being on the road a little less bad.

We are going home tonight after we finish our job and I can't wait. It's only a two hour drive, but as soon as we get back, I'm taking a shower, starting a load of laundry, and kicking back to catch up on some of my favorite shows.

Penny sent me a message earlier when she was at lunch, but I've been too busy to respond. I find it a little odd that Lucas never mentions whether or not she texts or calls him. He's never brought it up, so maybe she does, but I get the feeling that she doesn't, and I'm not sure why.

"We can get on the road in about 10 minutes," Lucas says to me as he finishes up some last minute things. "I don't know about you, but I'm ready to get out of these stiff, nasty things."

He pinches the front of his shirt and holds it out. My shirt is just as sweaty as his, so I know exactly how he feels. I'm glad that we packed up our hotel room this morning because I'd hate to have to go do it now. I'd probably sleep here another night before making the drive if it meant a shower and clean clothes, but we're pros at this and always do it the last morning of the job.

Lucas climbs into the driver's seat and buckles up before looking over at me. I have my phone in my hand, texting Penny. He smiles and nods.

"Is that our sweet little honey?" he asks.

"Penny?" I shake my head. "Yeah, I'm letting her know that we're on our way back, that away, she doesn't think she has to keep going to see my dad because we can go visit him tomorrow." He looks genuinely surprised as the corners of his mouth turn down. "What?" I ask.

"She visits your dad? Why does she do that?"

"I thought I told you," I say. "I don't know why she does it."

"There has to be some reason, Mason. What'd she say?" he presses.

Rubbing my temples as he gets on the highway, I sigh. "I don't know. I know that her dad was never around, so maybe it makes her feel good to be around a dad who gave a shit."

"Well, hell," he laughs, slapping the steering wheel. "If she's got daddy issues, I can help cure those."

While Lucas might be laughing, he's dead serious. He's into playing those daddy/dom roles. It's one of his favorite things to do. Most of the girls we've met have them so it wouldn't surprise me if Penny fits into that category. She was awfully tight-lipped about her family, especially when it came to her dad.

"Yeah, we know how that goes," I say. "The thing is, most of these girls who have daddy issues aren't as independent and secure as she is, and it kind of has me stumped about her. She's definitely different."

"Different? How?" he asks, weaving in and out of traffic, so we get home faster.

"It's hard to put my finger on it. She doesn't act like the others."

"Maybe. I haven't spent much time with her, not like you have," Lucas says. "What's she like anyway?"

It dawns on me that we haven't talked much about her since we left home, which is surprising. Usually, the two of us discuss how long we think a girl will last or whether or not she's into us. Penny's definitely into us. If she wasn't, why would she stick around?

"She's cool. I think what makes her different is that she's smart, like really smart, and she has a personality."

Lucas laughs. He knows exactly what I'm referring to when I talk about her personality. "You mean she's not a complete airhead," he says. It's a statement, not a question. "Those types are nice. So why do you think she's into us if she's so different from the other girls? I mean, if she's as smart as you say she is and has this great personality, why isn't she taken?"

I've been wondering the exact same thing myself. Penny's a good catch—for any guy. She's gorgeous, has a great body, a nice sense of style, and is intelligent. While we were at her apartment, I couldn't figure out why a girl like her would even consider guys like Lucas and me. Indeed, there have to be some good looking college grads that she could hook up with, get a nice ride and have a comfortable life.

Lucas and I bust our asses for the cash we make—which is excellent money—but we're not into psychology, science, and all that other stuff people go to college for; we're the opposite. We work in stiff jeans, sweaty shirts, and dirty boots—all of which I can't wait to get out of the minute we get home.

The more I think about it, Penny could land a guy who wears a suit and tie with Armani dress shoes. What is she doing with us?

"I'm not sure why she isn't with someone. You know, at first, I thought she was in a relationship or something. Maybe she was just cheating on her boyfriend or whatever, but when I was at her apartment, I knew that wasn't the case. There were plenty of pictures and lots of stylish designs, but it seemed....empty."

"Wait? You were in her apartment? When did you go there? What was it like?"

I know I mentioned this to him, didn't I? How could I not have told him about going to her place?

"I thought I told you?"

He shakes his head, "Nope. This is the first time I'm hearing about it."

"It's just an apartment with pictures here and there, lots and lots of books, a whole array of CDs and DVDs. We had to swing by her place before we went to see my dad. That's how she got into the whole visiting my dad thing."

"Oh! I remember now," he says. "It was when I brought Mandy home. She stayed over, and you two were gone before Mandy and I got out of bed. Did you bang her?"

His question makes me laugh. When have I not banged a hot girl in my bed?

"You could say that," we bump fists. "I can't believe we haven't talked about any of this."

"Dude, we've been working our asses off. There hasn't been time to talk."

He's not wrong. Work has been chaotic, and by the time we get off, we're too tired to talk so we just head to the bar, kick back with a couple of cold beers, order whatever shitty bar food they're serving up, and then go back to the hotel. This might be one of the first trips in a long time where we didn't score any chicks, and my body can tell. I hope Penny comes over as soon as we get back. Well, not as soon as we get there, but after I've had a chance to wash the film off my skin and put something clean on.

"Where'd you find that Mandy girl?" I ask.

He shrugs his shoulders. "She was at some after-party that I went to and was pretty lit. We hung out for a while, and she was all over me, so I brought her home, but she's kind of crazy."

Lucas is a magnet for the crazy chicks, so it doesn't surprise me, but I am curious how crazy he's talking about.

"What'd she do? She wasn't crawling around like a cat was she?"

The last time he brought home a stray, she literally crawled around on his bed, hissing, and pawing at him like she was a fucking cat. He ended up calling her a cab and told her never to come back.

He rolls his eyes, but I know he's picturing that chic. "No, she kept mumbling shit in her sleep. She was saying stuff like, 'No, no more meds!' and fighting the air."

Laughing my ass off, I say, "I don't know how you find these girls, but I'm glad it's not me."

The rest of the drive home is silent as the sunset begins to fade and the moon begins to come out. The minute we enter the house, I immediately start a shower. "I'll take a quick one so you can have one, too," I say to Lucas who's sorting the mail.

"Go ahead. I'm going to see about having some food delivered while you're in there, so, hopefully, by the time I get out, we can eat."

After my shower, I text Penny to let her know that we're home and to see if she wants to hang out. Lucas and I could definitely use the touch of a woman after being on the road, and Penny's just the woman who can give it to us.

In a strange twist, I actually miss her. I know that I didn't say it back to her on the phone, but I can't. Things get too complicated when we let emotions get involved, so it's better to keep it simple. Lucas and I made a pact to share everything—including girls.

It's easier that way, to share things, and it's a lot of fun.

Lucas is my best friend, and I love sharing girls with him. It's like we have this special bond that requires trust and loyalty; it's a much higher degree than that of a typical best friend relationship. We both have to follow the rules, or it won't work, and we're both very good at following the rules. That's not to say that we can't have solo nights with the woman we're sharing. Otherwise, I wouldn't have been able to enjoy Penny by myself before we left.

The only way that we wouldn't share a girl is if one of us met her on our own, and she was never shared between the two of us because that's an entirely different type of relationship, but I can't think of a time that that's ever happened. Penny certainly doesn't fall into that category, and she's too fun not to share. We make a good trio, and I wouldn't change one thing about it.

CHAPTER THIRTEEN

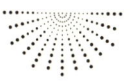

PENNY

I'm sitting in my apartment, studying, like I do every night, when my phone goes off with a text from Mason asking if I want to come over to hang out. Of course, I say yes because I've been bored and feeling a bit neglected since he and Lucas left for work weeks ago.

There have been a few times that I wanted to go out, but I haven't because I don't know what we are and I don't want to cause any ill feelings, so I've just sat at home like a good girl or went and visited Mason's dad.

That man absolutely adores me, by the way. Every time I go, we have such a good time. Mason is fortunate to have had a dad like him, and he's told me some hilarious stories about Mason's childhood. That boy got into so much trouble, and I can see it. He's a bit of a risk-taker, a dare devil, and likes to live on the edge.

I suppose that's why he and Lucas are such good friends. They're very much alike. It's strange, though. As much as I like Mason, I also like Lucas. It's just that I like Mason more. He's so much more personable than his friend, and we get along great. I know that they share things, including girls like me, but I'm not really sure how I'm supposed to act when I go over there.

Am I supposed to be Mason's....girlfriend? Are we even a thing? Or am I supposed to be there with the two of them? Things are so confusing.

Pulling on a clean t-shirt, I slip on my jeans, and slide my feet into my boots. My hair is a mess, and I have no makeup, so I run a brush through my tangled mess of a mop and apply a little foundation and some mascara.

When I pull up in front of their house, a pizza guy is leaving the house, hopping down the porch steps two at a time. We nod at each other before I knock on the door. Mason opens and smiles.

"Come on in. We just ordered some pizza, would you like a slice?"

I haven't eaten since lunch at school today, which wasn't very good, and the smell of the pizza makes my stomach growl.

"Sure," I say, taking a paper plate from him. "What's on it anyway?"

"Everything," says Lucas as he walks out of the bathroom, wrapped in a towel. "Don't eat it all!"

He walks into his room and shuts the door, emerging minutes later wearing a pair of sweats that hang low on his lean hips. I never realized how muscular he is, but he has a lot of muscle tone with great definition that pairs well with his tan skin.

"This is good," I say, taking another bite, trying to chomp off the gooey cheese from the crust.

"It's Imo's, what did you expect?" Mason laughs.

Imo's has always been my favorite pizza place. I remember when they started selling their products in the local grocery stores, I was so happy.

"I'm going to grab a beer," Lucas says, standing up. "Do you guys want one?"

Mason and I look at each other before nodding.

"I'm going to go see my dad tomorrow," Mason says as we hear Lucas clinking bottles around in the fridge. "Do you want to go with me?"

"Yeah, actually, I told your dad I was already coming," I nod.

"You did?"

"Is that a problem?" I ask.

"No," he shakes his head. "Not at all, I just figured that once I got back, you could use a break. I know how hard it is going to see him."

Lucas returns with four bottles of beer. Mason looks at him in question with the extra bottle. "I'm thirsty," he shrugs.

"It's not hard," I say. "Well, maybe for you, but not for me. I like visiting him. He's been telling me stories about you growing up."

"Oh God," Mason groans. "What did he tell you?"

"Let's just say that I know how when you were little, you thought you were like Superman since you had a cape and jumped off the roof of your house, and how you used to try sneaking girls into the house when you thought he wasn't paying attention."

Mason puts his head in his hands. "Why did he tell you that?"

"I guess because he likes me. Actually, he told me that he did."

"Yeah, that sounds like my dad. Thanks again for visiting him. I know you're busy with school and stuff."

"Really, it's not a problem," I say.

We're almost finished with our pizza and are all on our second beer because the sausage has been extra spicy tonight when Lucas pipes in and joins the conversation.

"Penny, I'm hurt," he says, holding his chest. "Why is it that Mason gets all this alone time with you and calls and messages, but I don't?" He gets up out of his chair to come sit on the other side of me, putting me between the two of them. "It's not fair that I don't have your number. We share everything, remember?"

He places his hand on my knee and slowly begins to slide it up my thigh. My eyes are focused on his hand, and my body instantly starts to react to his touch. Mason joins him by doing the same thing to my other leg, slowly moving his hand up my inner thigh until both of their hands meet at my crotch.

"We've missed you, Penny," Mason says, grabbing my pussy through my jeans.

I can already feel myself getting wet, and they've barely touched me. I feel like such a slut at how easily my body reacts to the two of them. I should be ashamed, but I'm not.

Lucas's hand continues, sliding under my shirt until he grips my breasts. My nipples immediately stand on end at the thought and feel of him touching me. Mason's hand is still where he left it, right on my crotch, rubbing me through my jeans.

Mason leans in, putting his mouth near my neck, making me turn my head to the side to grant him access as he begins sucking and kissing my throat. Lucas takes this opportunity to start kissing me, a deep, passionate kiss that we've never shared and it's fantastic.

My body feels electrified with both of them stimulating me, each in their own ways. Mason begins working on taking off my jeans while Lucas continues kissing me, massaging my breasts as he squeezes my nipples.

Slipping out of my jeans, Lucas pulls my shirt over my head, leaving me exposed between them wearing nothing but my panties and bra. I should feel vulnerable with the two of them staring down at me, their cocks hard and wanting, but I don't. I feel empowered.

Mason grabs the thin sides of my lace panties and pulls them down, leaving them around my thighs as he dips his finger inside me. My body betrays me, giving me away. I'm thoroughly wet, and we've barely begun.

"Already so wet," he says, removing his fingers from me, tasting my excitement.

Licking one finger at a time, he saves the last one for me and shoves it in my mouth. Greedily, I suck his finger, eager to taste myself on him.

"Let me see," Lucas says.

Repeating what Mason just did, he sticks his fingers inside me and removes them. This time, he makes me suck the first finger clean and tastes the rest for himself.

"Turn over," Mason orders.

I oblige, and roll over on top of Lucas, who begins kissing me immediately as Mason wastes no time pulling my panties the rest of the way off. With my attention focused on Lucas, Mason spreads my legs and places the head of his cock right against my entrance.

Gasping, I wait for him to enter, but he wants to play games. Sliding the wet tip of his cock—that's covered in my juices—he moves it back and forth between my clit and my opening. I'm dying for him to be inside of me, but he won't give it to me just yet.

Lucas breaks our kiss and grabs my hair, forcing me to look up at him. "Do you like being shared?" he asks.

Staring into his eyes, I can't answer him. I don't want to answer him, but Mason presses his cock against my entrance, allowing the tip to barely slide in and I want more.

I need more.

"Do you like it?" he asks again.

All I can think about is how good Mason's cock would feel buried deep inside of me, filling me and stretching me, but I know if I don't answer, he won't give me what I want.

Biting my lip, I say, "Yes," and just as I hiss the last sound, Mason pushes himself all the way inside of me.

CHAPTER FOURTEEN

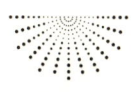

MASON

I knew she would say yes. We've never had a girl give us any other answer. She held out longer than I thought she would, though.

Judging from her wetness, she's been ready for this; waiting for this. They're all the same. Once you get a taste of this, it's hard to accept anything else.

Her pussy is so tight, it's gripping my cock, holding onto it. I nod at Lucas, who moves right on cue. Taking his dick out, he pushes Penny's head down on it, and she eagerly accepts as I start fucking her greedy, wet pussy.

Holding onto her sides, I work my cock until I'm balls deep, and that's when she really has trouble concentrating on giving Lucas head. She stops for a moment, making his eyes light up. He loves dominating girls with daddy issues.

Whether or not Penny has daddy issues doesn't really

matter, because to Lucas, it's all the same. He'll dominate any woman who will submit to him.

He reaches across her torso, and I watch as he raises his hand up in the air before letting it crash down on her ass. She yelps a little but gets right back to sucking his cock. Smiling, he admires his cherry red handprint that's on her ass while he pushes her head down to take him further.

Gagging, she tries to fight him, but she gives up quickly. I don't know what it is but I love it when he does that to girls, it turns me on to see him getting his dick sucked while having girls gag on it; but, for some reason, I want him to be easy with her.

I give him the signal to switch things up, which is the only reason he allows Penny to stop sucking his cock.

The two of us grab her and maneuver her so that she's flat on her back and he goes between her legs while I stand over her head. Lucas is rough with her, not even giving her a minute to accommodate his size before he stuffs her full with his long, thick cock as I occupy her mouth.

Needy, she reaches up and takes me into her mouth, sucking and deep throating my cock. She's so fucking good at what she does. She takes all of it like a good girl and even ends up gagging on it as I push my way past her tonsils and slide down the back of her throat.

I watch her full, round breasts bounce with each thrust that Lucas delivers. Her rosebud colored nipples are fully erect and hard, her legs spread wide open, taking every last inch of Lucas's cock. Looking down into her eyes, I see something there.

It must be the way she's looking at me, but it's more than lust and want. There's an attachment, almost like a connection.

As we stare into each other's eyes, I notice her shallow breathing and her face flush as she begins to come. The familiar shaking begins to return as Lucas brings her to a full orgasm. Her soft whimpers and pleading eyes are enough to push me over the edge.

Looking back over at Lucas, I watch him grab Penny's thighs and squeeze as he empties his balls in her. That coupled with the fantastic blowjob Penny delivers, I lose it before I have a chance to think about it and come right down her throat. She sucks me clean, swallowing every last drop, and doesn't release me until I start to go limp.

Lucas smacks her thigh as he whistles, "Damn girl, that was so good. I could do that all the time. Am I right?" he asks me.

"It was so fucking good," I say. "Too good." Leaning down, I kiss her on the forehead. "How was it for you?"

Smiling, she stands up and says, "I'm going to have to agree with you, it was too damn good."

"That's right," I smack her sweet ass before I watch it as she walks away, disappearing into the bathroom.

Lucas and I flop down on the couch, sipping our beer while Penny cleans herself up. "She's the best we've had in a while," he says.

I nod in agreement because it's true. "I've thought all along that she's different from the others."

Penny walks out of the bathroom, pulling her shirt down to cover herself until she slips back into her clothes. The two of us watch her dress herself; she has the perfect body, so it's near impossible to look away from her.

"Well, I'm out of here," Lucas says, getting off the couch.

"What? Why?" I ask. After the day we had, I don't know how he has the energy to move another muscle in his body. I'm beat and just want to climb into bed, watch some TV, and go to sleep.

"Party," he says. "There's one over on the East Side. Do you two want to go?"

I look at Penny who shakes her head no. "No, it's okay. You go ahead and go," I say. "Don't fall asleep behind the wheel. We've been up since the crack of dawn; I don't know how you do it."

"I won't fall asleep," he says, zipping up his jeans. "I'm the fucking Energizer Bunny. I just keep going, and going, and going." He beats an imaginary drum as he marches to the door and grabs a baseball cap off the hook. "Later, brother."

Penny and I have a good laugh as soon as the door shuts. "Is he always like that?" she asks.

"Lucas?" I shake my head. "He never stops. So, what do you want to do? Do you want to hang out, go back home, or what?"

She snuggles up to my side, resting her head on my shoulder as her finger traces the outline of my chest. "I want to hang out. You look exhausted, though."

I nod, "That' because I am. I'd suggest we Netflix and chill, but we already did the chill part. How about some TV and we go to bed?"

She cocks her eyebrow, pushing out her bottom lip, "Just go to bed?"

Wrapping my arm around her, I kiss her. "We'll see. Come on, let's go get in bed." Hand in hand, we walk to my bedroom and climb under the blanket together as I flip on the TV. "What do you want to watch?"

Nestling her head against my chest, she looks up at me with those gorgeous, heavy-lidded eyes and says, "I don't care. I'm not really here to watch TV, I just want to be with you."

CHAPTER FIFTEEN

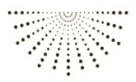

PENNY

Lying in Mason's arms, I feel so conflicted. I don't know what to say or what I should be feeling about all of this. I love being with both of them, but Mason's the one I really want to be with, and I'm curious if he feels the same connection that I do.

It's always the two of us who talk, hang out, and spend time together. Lucas just seems like he's in it for the sex, but Mason's much different. He puts forth an effort to have a relationship and takes time to get to know me. Lucas is always running off to the next party or chasing after the next girl, but Mason? He stays right here with me.

"You just want to be with me, huh?" he leans over and kisses my cheek, stroking my hair.

"Mhmm," I purr, snuggling up to him. He flips through the channels, but there's nothing good on TV. "I have a confession to make."

Smiling, his eyebrow ticks up. "Oh yeah? And what would that be?"

Rolling onto my stomach, I lay across his chest, looking into his hazel eyes. I'm afraid to tell him what I want to say because I don't know how he'll take it, but I think he should know how I feel.

"I really like you," I say, biting my lip.

"I like you, too," he says squeezing my ass with a playful grin still on his lips.

"No," I sit up on my elbows. "Like, I really like you." The smile fades from his face, so I continue. "Mason, I don't know if I can keep doing this anymore."

"Doing what?" his face scrunches.

"This. I don't know if I can keep doing this," I say, nodding toward the living room where the three of us just fucked. "I know that you guys have done this plenty of times and that you're used to it, but I'm not. I've never been in anything like this before, but I do know that I want to be with you."

He stops surfing through the channels and sits up in bed, propping himself against the headboard. His long, tan body still takes up the entire length of the bed, and his toned feet stick out from the bottom of the covers.

"Penny," he says. "I'm not sure where you're going with this, but Lucas and I share everything. We made that clear up front."

"I know you guys do 'stuff' together," I say, making an air quote around the word stuff. "But what happens when things turn into more than that? I know you can feel it, too. Every time we're together, I can feel it because I feel the same way, too."

"No," he shakes his head. "That's not how this works. Maybe we didn't explain things well enough to you."

Sitting up in bed, I scoot my feet under my bottom and face him. "Then tell me, Mason, because I'm so confused. What are we? What are we doing here?"

"What are we?" He echoes my question. "We're not anything, Penny. We can't be. Lucas and I made a pact a long time ago. Either of us are free to date whomever we'd like to date, but once we share a girl, we always share that girl. It's just how things are, and it works. It has always worked."

I hear the words coming out of his mouth, but they don't match his body language or facial expression. He says them as though he's reciting it from memory.

"So we can never be together? Just you and me?"

He reaches up, stroking my hair and takes a lock of it in his hands, twirling it around his fingers. "I'm sorry, but that's the way it is. I like you, I do. I really care about you, but I thought you understood that."

Hot tears are threatening to spill down my cheeks. I can't believe what I'm hearing; I thought he felt the same connection that I feel, but apparently, I was wrong. He doesn't feel the same about me at all, maybe it was all in my head. I want to leave; just get out of this bed, go, and never look back. I can't believe how foolish I've been.

"Listen," he says, his voice cracking as he clears his throat. "I don't want to lose you. I'm sure Lucas doesn't want this to end either. We've talked about you, and we both agree that you're good for us. Don't make me choose." I can't even look at him right now because if I do, I know I'll start crying. "Please," he adds.

Pushing his hand away, I scoot out of bed and stand up. "I'm sorry, I have to go."

Without another word, I walk into the living room and begin putting my boots on and grabbing my keys when he comes out of the bedroom after me. "Penny, wait."

"No, Mason. It's okay, really. I've got to go."

Slipping out into the night, I hop in my car and take off as tears begin to trickle down my face. I was so stupid to think that he liked me, or that we could ever be anything together as a couple.

By the time I get home, I'm exhausted. It's been a long day, and crying didn't help any, so I make myself a cup of warm chamomile tea and climb into bed. Maybe tomorrow will be better. I'll go to my classes, focus on my school, and forget that Mason and Lucas ever happened.

CHAPTER SIXTEEN

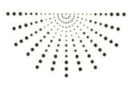

MASON

Penny has consumed my thoughts since the moment she told me how she felt, but I don't know what to do. We've never met anyone like her, and it kills me to know that she's upset.

I never meant to hurt her feelings. The truth is, she does mean a lot to me. I've never met a girl who would take the time to go sit with my dad or see to it that things were taken care of when I'm not around.

Maybe this is all my fault for spending so much time with her, especially without Lucas, but it was never my intention to hurt her. That's the last thing I want to do. Honestly, if we hadn't met her that night at the bar and took her home together, she would be a girl that I'd date, but once we share a girl, that changes everything.

I pour myself another bowl of frosted flakes and

continue my pity parade for misleading Penny and potentially fucking things up. I have to explain all of this to Lucas because he's going to question why she doesn't come around anymore.

Adding more milk to my bowl, I watch Lucas leave his bedroom to walk across the hall to the bathroom. He's in there for a good half hour as I finish my cereal before the toilet flushes and he walks out.

Placing my dishes in the sink, I scrunch my face at him. "You're disgusting," I say.

"What?" He asks.

"You didn't wash your hands."

He holds his hands up. "What? They're clean," he says defensively.

"Dude, you took a shit and didn't wash your hands. That's nasty."

"Here," he walks over to the sink and pumps some soap into his hands as he turns on the water. "Does this make you feel better?"

He dries his hands by wiping his shirt which makes me cringe. I don't know how I put up with him sometimes.

"What now?" he asks as I stare at him with my shoulders scrunched up around my neck.

"Why can't you use paper towels like a normal human being?"

"Okay, what's going on?" he says, plopping into a kitchen chair.

"What do you mean what's going on?"

"Mason, you're nitpicking everything I do. You look like something's bothering you, and you were up all night. So, tell me what's going on."

How the hell does he know that I was up all night? He's not wrong. I spent most of the night on the porch until he got home, and then I was in my room watching shitty infomercials. The shit they sell on TV amazes me these days, and why anyone would buy it is beyond me.

"What makes you think I was up all night?" I ask.

"For starters, you never sit out on the porch until two in the morning, you were blaring shitty commercials that I know you hate watching, and it's," he looks at his watch, "almost one in the afternoon and you're not dressed. Call me crazy, but usually by this time of day on our day off, you're at the nursing home feeding your dad."

Damn. He's right, but what else should I expect from my best friend? He knows me better than anyone; anyone, besides Penny. She knows me pretty well, too. I know I have to come clean about her to him, but I don't want to be to blame for fucking things up.

"Mason?" he presses, waiting for an answer.

"Fine," I say, my voice coming off harsher than I meant it to be. Looking out of the small, rectangular kitchen window, I see the sun reflecting off the chain link fence that encloses the backyard. A brown pigeon is hopping along the railing of the fence as though it's happy to be there.

Plopping down in the seat next to him, I lean over the table, taking my hand through my hair. "It's about Penny."

"What about her?" He asks. "Is she all right? Did something happen?"

"Yeah, something like that." I look him in the eye and study his face. He's beginning to worry. "We lost her."

"What do you mean we lost her? Lost her how?"

"She doesn't want to do this anymore; us. Said she couldn't handle it. I think she wants a real relationship, you know?"

He nods and looks out the kitchen window; the pigeon is gone like it had never been there, just like Penny. It's like she was never here. The house is so empty without her. We've spent the past 17 out of 20 Saturday's together—not that I was counting—and now she's gone.

"That sucks," he says. "Did she say why? I mean, what did she say to you?"

I don't want to tell him the truth, so I shrug my shoulders. Silence is better than telling him what really happened.

"You know what they say: all good things must come to an end," I say to him.

"Yeah, but that fucking sucks. She was perfect. Perfect body, perfect personality, perfect girl for us to share; damn, Mason, she was perfect in every way."

Hearing Lucas talk about her like this surprises me. He's not one to talk much about any of the girls we've shared. She must have left quite a mark on him, too. I can see the disappointment written all over his face.

The two of us sit in silence, staring out of the small kitchen window as we watch a couple of cars drive down the alley behind the house. I imagine he's thinking about things; I know that I needed time to do the same thing, but I took all night. He's just now learning that she's gone. It sucks being in his place right now.

"Listen, I do need to go see my dad today. Are you going to come with me?" I ask.

He bobs his head. "Let me take a shower first and then we can go." He makes it to the bathroom door when he stops and says, "Hey! Your dad's going to wonder where she is, so you'd better have a story ready for him or something because he really liked her."

Shit, my dad. I didn't even think about how losing Penny would affect him.

CHAPTER SEVENTEEN

PENNY

It's been almost two weeks since I've seen Mason or Lucas, and it's been the loneliest two fucking weeks. I haven't been this bored or lonely since....Owen. The thought of my boring weekends with Owen makes me laugh. At least when we were together, I had someone to talk to, but now I don't have anyone.

The only thing I've been able to do is bury myself in my school work, which is probably for the best. My whole life has been busy chasing the opposite sex. It's nice to put myself first for a change; it's been a long time coming. I figure once I'm finished with school and stable, I can look into dating, but for the time being, I'm finished with men.

I do miss Masons' dad, Bill, though. He's such a sweet man, and I've been wondering how he's doing, but I can't go see him. There's too much of a risk of running into

Mason on the weekends, and I also don't want to upset his dad by randomly showing up in case shit goes south and I'd have to stop seeing him for good, so it's better that I just stay away.

Neither Mason nor Lucas have tried to get a hold of me, which kind of surprises me. We had a good thing going, but I guess I shouldn't be too shocked. It's not like either one of them were serious about me. We were a good trio, the three of us, and it was fun while it lasted. God, do I miss it, though. We had so many good times.

When I first met those two, I never dreamed in a million years that it would've worked—especially as long as it did—but we were great together. Maybe I read too much into what Mason and I shared, but at the time, I felt it was real. I thought there was a connection between the two of us.

I suppose that I could've easily thought the same thing about Lucas if we had spent more time together like I had with Mason. It's hard for me to think that, though, because Lucas was always chasing after the next girl. I don't think he would've ever taken me seriously.

Exhausted from a long week, I decide to treat myself to a hot soak in the tub. Yep, just me, a couple of bath bombs, water hot as hell, and silence. For the past couple of weeks, my brain hasn't shut off. My thoughts have been non-stop, and I've made myself so busy that I've hardly had a moment to myself to do anything. Right now, I'm going to do absolutely nothing and not think about a single thing because I deserve it.

Running my water, I plop in two of my favorite bath bombs and grab a towel and a washcloth. It's been so long since I've pampered myself that it really does feel like a treat. Just to add more calmness for my soak in the tub, I light a vanilla-scented candle and climb into the water.

The steam swirling around me allows me to relax and clear my head. Placing my toes on the faucet, I see that my feet are in dire need of a pedicure. It's been ages since I've gone to the little shop down on 13th Street. They probably don't even remember who I am anymore.

Looking at my fingernails, I see that they could use a little TLC, too. I've never been one to keep up on that kind of stuff; there's just never enough time. Plus, with nursing school, they don't like us to have our nails painted, so it's not like I should really care too much about them right now anyway.

It doesn't take too long before the skin around my fingers and toes begin to shrivel like a prune from the hot water, which is starting to cool, so I reach for my towel and hear the loudest banging on my apartment door that I've ever heard in my life.

Jumping, I grab the towel and quickly start to dry off as I yell that I'm coming, but the banging is relentless.

"Hold on!" I shout.

Scared, and a little annoyed, I wrap the towel around me and head for the door. Looking through the peephole, I see Lucas standing on the other side of it.

"What are you doing here?" I ask, my heart pounding out of my chest as I crack the door.

"Hello to you, too, Penny. Aren't you going to invite me in?" Frowning, I glance down at my towel before looking him in the eye. "Oh, come on, Penny. I've seen you naked in positions that shouldn't even be possible."

Scared to death that my neighbors across the hall might hear him, I grab his shirt and pull him inside my apartment. "What are you doing here?" I demand.

Lucas ignores my question as he struts into my living room and looks around.

"Mason was dead on when he told me what your place looked like," he says after a beat.

Pulling my towel around me, I tuck it in a little tighter as I cross my arms. "Mason? He told you what my apartment looked like?"

He laughs, picking up a picture of Sabrina, Abby, and me. "Well, since I never got an invitation to come over, somebody had to tell me what your place looked like."

"Lucas, what are you doing here?" I finally ask again.

"I came to talk to you."

"Now isn't a good time. You could have at least called first," I huff.

He plops down on my couch and stretches his arms across the back of it like he owns the damn thing. I'm two seconds away from kicking him out of my apartment when he puts his dirty work boots on my table, and says, "I would have—if you would've given me your number."

I'd given him my number....hadn't I? Surely, at some point over the course of the last almost six months, we talked or texted. Right?

"Let me get dressed," I say. "I'll be right back."

Throwing on a pair of black leggings and a long, loose-fitting top, I head back out to the living room where I find Lucas musing around my apartment. Checking out my book collection, he seems either impressed or intimidated; I can't tell which.

"Find anything interesting?" I ask.

"He wasn't wrong about you. You love your books. What's this one about?" He holds up a paperback copy of We Were Liars.

"You didn't come here to ask me about books," I say, snatching it from his hand and putting it back on the bookshelf.

"No, I didn't, Penny. I came to talk to you about us."

"About us?" I'm not sure if I like where he's going

with this. I'm not sure who the 'us' is that he's talking about.

"Look, I know that you said you were done and we respect that but damn it, Penny. We want you back. We need you back."

"Why? Can't get any other girls to play your little game? The pact you two made?"

He cocks his eyebrow and tilts his head. "How do you know about our pact?" The look on his face tells me that I'm not supposed to know their rules, but I do. For a second, I regret saying anything because I don't want to cause a rift between him and his best friend, but he quickly forgets it. "It doesn't matter," he says. "The important thing is that we want you to come back."

"Both of you want me to come back? Why isn't Mason with you?"

He could be at the nursing home visiting his dad, but if they both wanted me so badly, I'm sure he could've left the nursing home a few minutes early to come with Lucas.

"I don't know what his deal is, Penny. Ever since you left, he's been different." His tone is concerning to me, so I let him continue instead of pushing him out the door even though I'm still annoyed by him. I want to know what he's got to say, especially if Mason's involved. "Things aren't the same without you."

"How?"

"For starters, he doesn't have you with him when he goes and sees his dad—,"

"How is his dad?" I cut him off. He pauses like he's not sure how to answer, and shrugs.

"He's been fucking up at work like he can't concentrate, he doesn't ever go out. I can't even tell you the last time I was able to drag his ass to a concert or party."

I laugh inwardly at the thought Lucas dragging Mason off to a party or concert. He's not the type. Instead, he'd rather go to a bar, shoot some pool or play darts, or sit around watching movies at home with a beer in his hand. Lucas is the party goer, not Mason.

"So, what do you want me to do? I mean, why are you here?"

Lucas glances aimlessly around my apartment as he scratches his stubble. It looks sexy on him; it's the perfect length. "I want you to come over tonight."

There's a bit of hopefulness in his voice like if he says it kind enough, I'll do as he wants, but I don't know if I can. I still want to be with Mason, and I still like Lucas. The trio thing was fun for a while, but I don't know if that's truly what I want. I've never been that girl, but God do I miss them.

I miss both of their hands on me, both of their mouths kissing me, and fucking both of their cocks. The two of them drive me insane when we're in bed. It's been weeks since I've been laid and truth be told, these two men have given me the best sex any woman could ask for.

Of course, it's not all about sex. I also miss their company, their laughter, their jokes, their....everything. Lucas's carefree spirit is just what I want, and Mason's heart is just what I need.

And it hurts me to know that Mason has been in a funk since I left. I understand their pact—sort of—so I can see why we can't be together but do I really want to be without him? Why should the two—or three—of us be apart, all suffering at the same time?

"I don't know if that's a good idea, Lucas," I say. I don't know how Mason will react if I go over there, and I'm almost afraid to find out.

"You have to, Penny. Please, I'm begging you. We can go back to the way things were. It'll be good, I promise."

Opening the door, I say, "I think you should go, Lucas."

Walking toward the door, he reaches out and cups my face with his hands. "Please, Penny." Lowering his face, he presses his lips against mine, kissing me before disappearing into the hallway.

I'm so torn, I don't know what to do. Maybe I'll go, maybe I won't.

CHAPTER EIGHTEEN

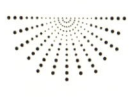

MASON

After visiting my dad, I feel bad that he's still asking for Penny. You'd think that he would've forgotten about her, given his mental state, but I have no such luck. It's been a couple of weeks now, and every time I see him, he asks, "Where's my pretty Penny?"

He's completely crazy about her, and I can see why. They spent a lot of time together and had so much fun. She must've told him a lot about herself while the two of them were hanging out because he remembers that she's going to school to become a nurse and that she'll graduate in the next few years. I've been lying to him, telling him that she has exams because it's better than saying she split.

I miss her and what we had, but it would never work: the two of us being a couple and me sharing her with my best friend. That's never been how we operate. I can't stop myself from wishing I would've met her sooner, before that night at The Impulse. Things would be so much different because, in my eyes, she's the perfect girl.

Turning the knob on the washing machine, a cold gust of air whips past me as I hear the front door shut and see Lucas tossing his keys on the table while he blows warm air into his hands. This winter has been so cold, which has really sucked for work. It's been flurrying off and on all day, and they're calling for snow tonight. The meteorologist said we might get up to seven inches, but I doubt it. It's the only job where you can consistently fuck it up and never be fired. I'm guessing we'll have more like three to four inches.

"Fuck, is there any coffee left from breakfast?" he asks.

"No," I shake my head. "There was only a little in the pot, so I dumped it before it had a chance to dry up and burn to the bottom of the glass."

"Then I'm starting some," Lucas says. "You want any?"

"Nah, I got something," I say, holding up a beer bottle. "Unlike you, I know how to keep my ass inside when it's below zero unless I have to go out."

He scoops some coffee grounds into the pot and hits

the button to turn it on. "Well, I'm not going out tonight, so that's got to count for something, right?"

"Whoa! Did hell freeze over? Did I just hear you say that you're staying in for the night? That never happens."

"Don't be a smart ass," he says. "There are no concerts, and the only party that I know of is going to be lame. Besides, I figured I'd hang out with my best friend. I have a surprise for you," he adds.

My eyebrows perk up; this is entirely uncharacteristic of himself. I love Lucas like a brother, but he's completely selfish. "A surprise? What is it?"

"You'll see," he says, walking into the bathroom, shutting the door behind him.

I don't know what he's got up his sleeve, but it's probably dumb. Knowing him, it's a couple of girls that he met somewhere, and I couldn't care less.

As evening falls, the snow begins to pick up. Sitting on the couch, I can hear tires spinning out, so I pull back the heavy blue curtains to look through the window. Surprisingly, there are about five inches of snow, and an old Camaro is turned sideways before it finally rocks itself out of the tire tracks it's stuck in and starts sliding down the street. Maybe the weatherman finally got it right, I think to myself.

Plopping back down on the couch, I continue watching The Voice when Lucas comes out of his bedroom and looks through the window. "It's coming down pretty good out there, isn't it?"

I nod, taking a sip of my beer, and continue watching TV. "Was that your big surprise? You knew it was going to snow?"

"No," he says. "You'll see, just wait."

Ignoring him, he finally leaves and goes into the kitchen. I laugh to myself thinking about what his surprise could be. For all I know, he's got a couple of babes coming over, but I'm not interested. I haven't been interested in any girls since Penny.

When Lucas comes waltzing back into the living room, there's a knock at the door, and a grin creeps across his face.

"I believe that's for you," he says, nodding toward the door.

Rolling my eyes, I sigh, "I'm not—,"

"Go on, open it," he cuts me off.

Reluctantly, I get off the couch and open the door. Penny's standing on the porch with snow lining the shoulders of her brown coat as she rubs her hands together in an attempt to warm them.

"Hi," she murmurs, looking into my eyes. It seems like it's been forever since I've seen those topaz gems of hers, and it's like a sight for sore eyes. "Lucas said—,"

"I said come on in," he blurts out. "It's cold as hell out there, and you're letting all the cold air in."

Stepping aside, I let her in the house. How he got her here is beyond me, but I'm so glad she's here. "Did you drive over here?" I ask, glancing at the street before shutting the door.

"Yeah," she says, sliding her coat off. "The roads are getting bad, but I saw MODOT salting the streets, so it should be fine."

"Would you like some coffee?" Lucas offers her. "I made some not too long ago, and it's still hot."

"Sure, that'd be great. Thanks."

Taking a seat on the couch, she sits right next to me, and I can't keep my eyes off of her. Her skin is paler than the last time I saw her and she looks like she's lost a few pounds. Maybe the last couple of weeks have been as hard as her as they were on me.

"How've things been going?" I ask her.

"Good, just been going to school and I've been hunting for a job at one of the hospitals so I can get my clinicals in. You?"

"I've just been freezing my ass off, working in the cold."

She nods, "How is your dad? Has he been doing okay?"

"He asks about you all the time," I laugh. "He calls

you his 'Pretty Penny,' and thinks you've been buried in studies."

"Aww, yeah, he was calling me that right before....you know," her voice trails off.

"You know what?" Lucas asks, returning with her coffee.

"Nothing, thank you."

Sipping her coffee, I realize how much I've missed sitting here talking to her. I'd be lying if I said our feelings weren't mutual, but I know how much Lucas likes her, too. He might not act like it, but he shows it in his own way and I could never throw away our friendship over a girl.

"Let me grab you a blanket," he says to her. "You're still freezing."

"I'm fine," she calls after him, but he throws his hand up in the air as he disappears to get a blanket for her.

I want to tell her how much I've missed her, but I know that now is not the time, so I keep my mouth shut.

CHAPTER NINETEEN

PENNY

"It's okay, Lucas. Really," I say as he fusses over me.

He brings out a fuzzy tiger-print blanket and lays it over the three of us as he takes a seat next to me on the couch. Just like old times, I'm sitting between the two of them on the couch. It feels awkward, yet familiar at the same time.

"We can't have our favorite girl getting cold, can we?" he says, winking at me.

"I don't think I'm a favorite," I say, looking toward Mason.

Instead of confirming or denying, he turns his glance back toward the TV. A few seconds pass by before Lucas blows the lid open and confronts the two of us.

"Come on, you two," he slaps his knee. "I don't know

what's going on between you because neither one of you will say a damn word, but I'm going to fix us something to eat while the two of you talk. I don't want what we had to go to waste so get your shit straightened out. Okay?"

Without another word, he gets off the couch, leaving me to face Mason all alone. I have no idea what we're supposed to talk about, so I don't say a single word.

"I know things aren't ideal, Penny, but he's right: we did have a good thing, the three of us, and if he invited you that must mean that he misses you as much as I do."

Hearing that Mason misses me makes my heart skip a beat. I never thought I'd listen to him say those words, even if he's not entirely confessing how much or little he's missed me.

"Lucas? Missed me?" I laugh. "He's the fastest bed hopper in the Midwest, there's no way he could ever miss anyone."

"Believe it or not, Lucas doesn't chase girls so if he came after you, it meant something. We meant something, and he's right. I missed you, too. We had an awesome thing going with the three of us." He pretends to watch TV for a moment before continuing. "I know I'd like to have you back."

I can't stop myself from smiling. "You would?"

"Of course, I would," he puts his arm around me and

kisses me. "We had a lot of good times together, and the sex was mind-blowing."

We both laugh because we know it's true. Sitting on the couch, we continue watching The Voice until Lucas comes back into the living room, covered in red pasta sauce.

"Did you two have a good talk? Dinner's ready."

"What the hell did you make?" Mason asks, pointing to Lucas's shirt. "A volcano?"

"No, I made spaghetti. Come eat."

Mason and I shoot each other sideways glances as we get off the couch. Following Lucas into the kitchen, it's a complete mess, and it doesn't smell like spaghetti; it doesn't smell good at all. I take a peek inside the pot, and it looks like spaghetti. Neither of us wants to offend him, so we scoop a pile onto our plates and have a seat at the table.

The noodles are undercooked, and it tastes bland. Nobody talks for the first few minutes until Lucas pipes up.

"This doesn't taste very good, does it?" he asks.

Mason and I look at each other and shake our heads no. "What did you put in it?" I ask.

"Hamburger, noodles, and sauce."

"And what else?"

"That's it," he says, pushing it around on his plate with his fork.

"I think that's the problem. You didn't season the meat," I say.

"Season the meat with what? Doesn't it get its flavor from the sauce?"

Laughing, I put my hand on his. "No, that's not how it gets its flavor. Do you have any more sauce or noodles? I can whip up something in about 30 minutes."

"Yeah, I only used half of what we had," he says.

"Okay, I'll make dinner. You two get out of here."

The guys head out of the kitchen, leaving me to clean the horrendous mess that Lucas made, but I don't mind. I'd rather be here with them than at my apartment by myself. I can't believe how easy it was to talk to Mason. He didn't dwell on the past or the last conversation that we had, and made it so easy to start over new.

About a half an hour later, I've got spaghetti made—real spaghetti, not the shit Lucas tried feeding us—so I call them into the kitchen.

"Oh, it even smells better in here," Lucas says as he walks in. "What did you do differently? How come my spaghetti didn't smell like this?"

I roll my eyes and laugh. "Well, if you're as good of a cook as Mason, it's because you don't know how to cook."

"What? What's that supposed to mean?" Mason jumps to his own defense.

"Oh, nothing," I say, my voice dripping with sarcasm. "It's just that I remember making your eggs and asking how you wanted them. Your answer was: can you make the yolks runny?"

"In my defense, I've never been given options," he says. "But I definitely like the way you cook."

While the three of us eat, we make light conversation about nothing in particular, and I love every minute of it. When we're done, we scrape our plates and toss them in the dishwasher.

"How about a game of dirty Scrabble?" Lucas suggests as we head back into the living room.

"I'm game," I shrug. "But just so you know, I'll probably kick ass and beat both of you."

"Ha!" Mason exclaims. "You haven't played with us before. We're really good at it."

We gather around the coffee table, and I go first. My letters completely suck, and I end up having to make the word 'bunt.'

"If that's all you've got, you'll be naked in no time," Lucas says, grinning as he arranges his tiles on the board. Using the u from my word, he makes the word 'uncle.' Mason's up next and makes the word 'lemons.'

Within 45 minutes, the guys are kicking my ass as the

snow outside continues to accumulate on the streets. We've all had to remove at least two articles of clothing, and I lose again.

"I think she should lose the shirt," Mason says. "Let's see what you've got under there." Grabbing my shirt, he gives it a slight tug.

"Nah, I think she should ditch the pants," Lucas grins. "I'm more interested in what's under them."

"I've got you both beat! Ha!" I say, sliding off my bra from under my shirt. "I'll keep my pants and my shirt."

The guys look at each other as they crack up laughing. "That's cheating!" Lucas says.

"Hey! The rules are you have to remove an article of clothing, there are no rules in which article."

"She's got you there," Mason says, toasting our beer bottles. "Besides, I like her braless."

I look down at my chest and see my nipples poking straight through the thin material of my shirt. "Oh, you guys are bad!" I laugh. "You should turn the heat up in here."

"No, I like it better this way," Lucas agrees with Mason. "Gives us a nice view."

Oh god. I put my head in my hand. This is precisely what I've missed, and I'm so glad I decided to come over tonight. I almost didn't, but I wanted to because I was hopeful that Mason would be his usual, and he didn't fail.

Another half an hour goes by, and now I have to decide: shirt or pants? I didn't think the guys would be this good, but they are. I thought I was so smart taking my bra off, but now I see the errors in my ways; I didn't think I'd lose this much.

"What will it be now?" Mason asks. Both of them have a smug look on their face like, "I told you so," but neither of them says a word because I already know.

"You know, you're not as slick as you'd like to think; neither of you are. Both of you are shirtless!" I've been staring at their sculpted chests for the last 20 minutes, and god do I miss touching them. They've both lost quite a bit of their tan since it's been winter, but they're still stunning.

"Yeah, but we weren't the smart-ass who decided to remove our bra. I vote shirt," Mason says.

"I would've voted for pants like I did earlier, but knowing that she doesn't have a bra on makes me want to vote for the shirt, too," Lucas grins.

"The hell with both of you," I huff. "I'll take off my pants, and then that will be the last piece that I remove because I'm making a comeback!"

"Right," Lucas says, waving his hand. "A comeback," he mocks me with air quotes. "Just take those pants off so we can see what pretty panties you have on tonight."

Sliding my jeans over my hips, I push them down and step out of them, exposing my lacy g-strings.

"Nice!" Lucas whistles. "Can't wait until those are on the floor, too."

Pursing my lips, I make a sour face at him, but, honestly, I can't wait either. I've been undersexed for weeks now, and these two are looking really damn good.

CHAPTER TWENTY

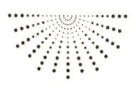

MASON

I can't stop staring at her. She's even more beautiful than I remembered. Her long, wavy blonde hair is flowing over her shoulders, and her pouty lips are begging to be kissed, but first, we're going to make her lose this game of dirty Scrabble.

We're almost finished with the game because Lucas is down to his last four letters, and I'm down to my last two. Penny has the most out of all of us. I don't know if she just had shitty luck tonight or if she purposely didn't use as many letters as she could, but we've been mopping the floor with her.

"And that means you have to lose either the shirt or the panties," Lucas says, scoring an insane amount of points with the word 'vacancy' because he got a triple letter score.

Penny looks to me for help, but I hold my hands in the air. "Don't look at me. A loss is a loss." She sticks her tongue out at me, mocking me as she mouths the words. "Although, I can help you remove one of them if you like."

Lucas catches on and joins in. "Yeah, me too."

The two of us stand up, enclosing her between us; Lucas is behind her, and I'm facing her. Closing the distance between the three of us, Lucas and I each step toward one another until there's no more space.

Reaching down, I grab the hem of Penny's top and begin slowly lifting it over her head as we stare into each other's eyes. It's like unwrapping a Christmas present on Christmas morning. I want to take my time and go slow, appreciating the gift, but I want to tear into it and finally have it. Lifting her shirt over her head, I toss it onto the couch, exposing her bare breasts.

Breaking eye contact, I look down and see her panties hit the floor as Lucas slides his hands back up her thighs, grabbing onto her hips as he kisses her neck from behind. Swallowing the sigh that escapes her pouty lips, I press my lips against hers and kiss her deeply. My cock instantly goes hard as she wraps her hands around the back of my head, pulling me closer to her.

Lucas and I maneuver the three of us into the bedroom and collapse on the bed together. With my lips still sealed against hers, we continue kissing as I rake my fingertips over her hardened nipples while we lie next to each other in our own world. I completely forget that we're not alone until she spreads her legs, resting her upper leg against my thigh as Lucas goes down on her. Soft whimpers escape her throat as his tongue traces circles around her clit.

A tinge of jealousy surges through me as I watch him between her legs, but I push it aside and concentrate on pleasing Penny because she's all that matters. For me, it's always been about pleasing the woman, especially when it comes to her.

Pulling her nipple into my mouth, I lightly bite it as I suck it until it's a perfect point before moving onto the other one. Tiny goosebumps break out around her areola as she pushes my head closer to her breasts. I gently squeeze them in the palms of my hands as I continue teasing her.

Closer and closer, Lucas pushes her to orgasm until she can no longer handle it and comes all over his face. For the first time ever, I'm envious that he made her come. Not only did he make her come, but she came for him before me. I should've been the first one to get her off.

"Move over," I say to Lucas, nudging him out of the way. "It's my turn."

Penny tries to push my head away, giggling, "No,

Mason, please. I'm too sensitive. Holy hell that was a good orgasm."

Refusing to take no for an answer, I begin peppering her inner thighs with soft kisses. "It's okay, I'll go easy," I promise. Melting into the mattress, Penny relaxes her legs, granting me full access. "There you go," I murmur, sliding my long tongue up the length of her pussy until I get to her clit.

Tracing the alphabet on her clit, I glance up and see Lucas beside her, kneeling next to her head as she takes his cock into her mouth. Another jab of jealousy cuts through me. She should've been sucking my cock first, not his.

This only drives me further to ensuring that I give her an even bigger orgasm than he did, and I know exactly how to push her buttons. Inserting my finger inside of her, I turn it upward so that my fingertip is facing the ceiling and begin working on her G-spot as I continue to lap up her juices and pay close attention to her clitoris.

Lucas has a hold of her head, pushing his entire dick down her throat, so I do everything I can to break her concentration and kick things up a notch. Fingering her, I begin nibbling and sucking on her clit as I continuously stroke her G-spot, harder and faster than before. Her legs start to shake and her back arches away from the mattress.

Glancing over the top of her freshly shaved pussy, I

see her hardened nipples and hear her moans filling the room. She's right there at the edge, and all she needs is a small push, and that's exactly what I give her. Her hips thrust in the air as her hands grab onto the blankets, twisting them, and knotting them up as she comes all over my face. I don't stop until her thighs clamp down on my head, threatening to pop it like a balloon, and she's begging me to stop.

Satisfied that she had a better orgasm with me than she did with Lucas, I stand up at the foot of the bed and grab her legs, wrapping them around me. My cock slides into her soaking wet pussy, and she feels so damn good. The walls of her pussy grip my cock like it's been waiting for it, and I eagerly give it to her. Pounding into her has never felt better until I see Lucas still enjoying her as she sucks his throbbing cock, and I know that feeling all too well.

Envious watching the two of them enjoy each other as she takes his cock and he plays with her breasts, I fuck her like she's never been fucked before, unleashing all of my jealousy, anger, and frustration.

Fuck this pact, I tell myself over and over with each thrust. Lucas begins to moan as Penny strokes his balls while sucking his cock until he begins to come, milking him for all he's got. For some fucked up, twisted reason, the sight of him getting off on her pushes me over the edge, and I lose it. I can feel my cock beginning to pulsate and throb as I shoot my hot cum inside her. Instead of letting up on her, I fuck her harder and harder until my balls are completely empty and I'm a sweating mess.

"Damn, bro," Lucas snickers as he grabs a shirt and pulls it over his head. "I've never seen you fuck so hard." He looks down at Penny and smiles as he smacks her thigh, "See? What'd I tell you? I told you he missed your ass!"

Guilt washes over me as I think about how much I care for Penny and how I let my best friend fuck her. Not only did I let him fuck her, but I got off on the fact that he was coming all over her face and tits while my dick was in her.

I wish we never brought her into this. I wish I never met her. Yes, I do, that's a lie. I'm so fucking grateful for the day she walked into my life—our lives—but damn it, I don't want to share her. I feel like I'm being selfish for wanting to keep her all to myself, but ever since she let the cat out of the bag about how she felt, I haven't been able to stop thinking about her; about us.

Penny sits up on the bed, still wiping Lucas's cum out of her hair while I watch myself drip out of her pussy. She instantly knows that something's wrong when she looks at me because I can see her thoughts reflected in her expression. I don't know if it's hurt, resentment, or sadness that we can't be together, but whatever it is, I know we can both feel it.

Pulling on my boxers and a pair of flannel pajama pants, our eyes lock. A million thoughts and emotions are running through my mind, but only one sentence leaves my mouth.

"I think it's time for you to go," I say to her, leaving her and Lucas in my room as I walk into the bathroom.

I don't care what she does, but she has to go. I can't keep doing this with her, and with Lucas. I can't watch the two of them together anymore. The jealousy was more than I could handle. She has to go tonight.

CHAPTER TWENTY-ONE

PENNY

Lucas looks at me, puzzled by what's going on. Obviously, he knows nothing about how Mason and I feel about each other. I should've known it was a bad idea to sleep with them again. I should've just stopped at coming over to visit and left it at that, but we were having so much fun. Before I knew it, one thing kind of led to another and we were all naked, having a great time.

"What's that all about?" Lucas asks me when the bathroom door slams shut.

"I-I don't know," I lie. The last thing that I want to do is cause friction between them. They've been best friends for so long; I don't want to ruin any more relationships than I already have. "I think I'm going to go ahead and take off."

Getting out of the bed, I make my way into the living room where my clothes are. The Scrabble board is still on the table, reminding me what a loser I am—in more ways than one.

"Penny, you can't go tonight," Lucas says as I put my pants and bra on. "It's been snowing its ass off all day and night, plus it's fucking freezing. What if you wreck or something? Just stay here tonight."

Shaking my head, I say, "No way. He wants me gone, so I'm out of here." My feelings are hurt because I don't want to go. I thought I was doing what would make them both happy, but it completely backfired on me. Even Lucas has the decency to let me stay the night because the roads probably are bad. "I don't want to stay where I'm not welcome." Slipping my boots on, I grab my coat and purse.

"Don't listen to him," he says. "Sometimes Mason gets stabby like that, but it'll be okay. He didn't mean it. Please, Penny, don't go."

"No, Lucas, I think coming over here was a mistake." I zip up my coat and put my gloves on. "I should've stayed home tonight. It was very foolish of me to come out in the bad weather, and silly of me to come over here without talking to Mason first." I open the door and see a thick blanket of white snow covering everything, including my car. "Goodnight, Lucas."

Kissing his cheek, I slip out into the biting wind. Snow flurries flutter through the air, landing on top of my coat and hair as I scrape the snow off my car. I can't tell if it's still coming down or if it's just the existing snow blowing through the crisp air, but I do know it's fucking cold and I hope that my car is warm because the tears streaming down my face feel like they could freeze.

I give Mason's house one last glance as I pull away from the sidewalk and see the living room light go out. I must be the dumbest girl in all of St. Louis for thinking something like this could work, or that I could have Mason all to myself.

When I get home, my feet and hands are frozen, but they're nowhere as cold as my heart feels at the moment. I feel so rejected, unwanted, and abandoned. It was a significant risk telling Mason my feelings in the first place, and he pushed me away. It was so stupid of me to go back there thinking that things would go back to being the way they were.

Even when Lucas and I were having fun, it didn't feel right, but in my mind, I felt that I had to include him to have Mason. It's not exactly what I wanted, but I guess it was wishful thinking that I could finally have Mason back in my life again.

Taking a steaming, hot shower, I let the water warm my body, but I can't get warm enough. I don't know if it's because I feel so cold on the inside or if it's because I was outside for nearly twenty minutes clearing off my car and letting it warm up in the blistering weather.

Putting on my fuzzy pajamas, I climb into bed and lie awake as I stare at the ceiling replaying tonight's events in my head. It went from good to excellent, to fucked up in a matter of hours. I might be crazy, but I could've sworn that Mason was hurting just as bad as I was. There was something in his eyes that resonated with me, but I can't put my finger on exactly what it was.

Drifting off to sleep, I keep thinking about the last time I saw him, how I watched him walk away from me and slam the bathroom door shut. Tears wet my pillow as I finally let go for the night and try to put it all behind me.

It's the last week of school, and I'm amazed at how fast time has flown by this year. I've been busy registering for my second year of nursing school and couldn't be more excited. I'll finally have my LPN license before I know it.

My savings was nearly depleted by the time I finally received my first job offer at St. Louis Regional Hospital. I started working there a couple of weeks ago, and I really like it. I'm hoping it will lead to better job opportunities once I'm actually licensed, but for now, I'll take what I can get. They've put me to work as a nurses aid in the intensive care unit. It's been challenging, but it will allow me to get some of the hands-on training that I need for school, plus allow me to replenish my savings account while still affording my apartment.

I haven't dated or even entertained the idea of dating since I last talked to Mason and Lucas. Neither one of them have reached out to me, and I've not bothered trying to talk to them. I guess it's better that way. It allows me to focus on myself, which is what I set out to do once things were over between Owen and me.

It sucks though, because I miss Mason. All right, I miss Lucas a little too, but only as a friend. He was always chasing the next skirt and always looking out for himself—not that there's anything wrong with that, but that's what set him and Mason apart.

Knowing that his dad called me his 'Pretty Penny' and was still asking for me haunts me to this day. With his mental state, he's probably forgotten who I am by now, which makes me happy and sad at the same time. I don't want him wondering where I went, but I also don't want him to forget who I was either. His dad was really cool, even for an old man in a nursing home. I know why Mason had to put him in there, but I hated seeing him lying in that bed.

Lately, I've been hanging out with Abby and Sabrina

when I'm not working or studying, but no matter how much we go out and they try to hook me up with guys from the club, I can't do it. I keep hoping that one day I'll find a guy as good as Mason and settle down, but I don't know if that's possible. He was so different from every other guy that I've met.

My lease is up at my apartment at the end of summer, so I've been weighing my options between living on campus or renewing my lease. There are pros and cons to both, I just have to figure out which one's right for me. I'm so tired of living alone, which makes me want to live in a dorm so I'll at least have some friends to hang out with, but it's tough. I have friends now, and I barely hang out with them, so I'm not sure sticking me in housing with a bunch of younger college kids is really the right answer.

I've got to start downsizing my costs, though, because school is expensive. That's another option that I've been toying with: getting a roommate, but I don't know if that's the right thing to do, either. I just wish that things could go back to the way they were at the beginning of this past school year when I was over Owen and ready to have some fun. Things were so much more relaxed then, and I didn't have to think about things too much.

I was content living in my own little bubble while going to school and having fun. Nothing was serious back then, but once I met Mason and Lucas, everything changed. I wish I could redo the snowy night with them before things became even more complicated.

Sometimes, I think about calling or texting Mason, but I figure what's the point? I'm probably the last person he wants to hear from.

CHAPTER TWENTY-TWO

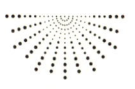

MASON

My life has been complete hell since Penny walked out of our lives. Knowing how much I cared about her, I should've never agreed to play a game of dirty Scrabble, but I figured it was harmless.

Never in a million years did I think I'd become that envious, that jealous of my best friend. We've had sex together so many times that it was just the norm, but then Penny walked in and tore it all apart.

She started by tearing down every wall in my heart. Hanging out with me, visiting my dad, going on fun little dates together—if that's what you want to call them—and being herself was all my downfall. She's such a beautiful person, inside and out. My chest still aches every time I think about her being gone from my life.

It's been four months since we last saw each other. I'd be lying if I said I didn't look for her when I'm at the supermarket or driving through traffic. Even though I was the one who ended things, I want her back so badly.

She's probably moved on, found some great college guy, or fell in love with a doctor. The thought of her dating another guy makes me want to kill a person. I don't know how I watched Lucas fuck her and use her body for his pleasure, or how I got off on it.

I've had a lot of time to think about this, and I don't think it was me getting off on my friend using her body. I think I got off on her sexuality, and how damn powerful she was in the bedroom. Out of all the women I've been with, Penny owns her passion. She might not be a dominant person, especially in the bedroom, but she's all woman.

There have been so many nights where I've lied awake in bed thinking about her and wondering how she's doing. I've had to stop myself from sending her a text or dropping by her apartment.

Work has kept me busy, which has helped immensely. Lucas and I have a big job that we're going to bid on this week, and I'm grateful for it. We're leaving for three days to go down to the boot heel of Missouri to get everything lined up for a new school they're building. Since it's summer, that should keep me from swinging by Penny's place now that I know she's out of college, too.

The job should take us the next couple of months, and by the time we get back, Penny should be gearing up to go back to school. My hopes are that's enough to keep me away from her.

Pouring myself a cup of coffee, I wait for Lucas to finish getting ready. The truck's all packed with our things, and we'll be hitting the road just as the sun is beginning to rise. Hopefully, we'll be in Hayti, MO just in time for lunch.

"Do you have everything you need?" Lucas asks, stepping out of his room.

I nod. "Yeah. Are you ready?"

He puts on his sunglasses, swings his duffel bag over his shoulder and says, "Let's go."

We load into the truck and set out south on Highway 55 just as the sun is peeking over the horizon. Looking in the side mirror, I watch St. Louis grow smaller and smaller until it disappears.

I hope Penny has a good summer; she deserves the best of everything, and I wish I could be part of it.

Rushing down the highway, I can't believe that my dad had another stroke. The nursing home called about an hour after we started work this morning. Lucas and I have only been on the job site for a week, and I hate to leave him there by himself, but I don't have any other choice.

My phone rings just as I pass Cape Girardeau.

"Hello?" I answer.

"Hello, Mr. Rogers? This is Karen, the nurse from your father's nursing home."

I recognize her voice immediately, considering that she was the one who notified me when he initially had his stroke. "Hi, yes, is everything okay?"

"I'm sorry," she says, her voice dropping an octave. "But your dad began having mini-strokes, and we had to rush him to St. Louis Regional Hospital. He should be arriving there momentarily, but I wanted to let you know so that you could go straight to the hospital instead of coming here."

"Mini-strokes?" I repeat. "Why?"

"It's hard to say, Mr. Rogers. There are a number of reasons that can happen. I'd advise you to get to the hospital as quickly as possible."

Pressing my foot harder on the accelerator, I speed down the highway. "I'm on my way."

I slam my fist into the dashboard as I hang up the call. "Damn it!" I yell.

Why does it have to be my dad? Why did it have to happen when I was a couple of hours away?

Anger and frustration build up inside of me as I coast down the highway. I think back to the last time I saw him, which was the day before we left. He told me he wasn't feeling well, but I figured it was the change in weather.

An hour later, I'm pulling into the first parking space I can find and dashing through the parking lot to the front door. I approach the older woman who's patiently sitting behind the desk.

"Can I help you, sir?" she smiles sweetly.

"I'm here to see my father, his name is Bill Rogers. William Rogers, he was brought in by ambulance for a stroke," I say, winded and out of breath.

She nods and knows exactly who I'm talking about. She's probably worked here a hundred years and knows everything, but I'm glad she here.

"Yes, William Rogers is in ICU on the third floor. When you get there, one of the nurses will show you to his room."

Hopping on the elevator, I feel my heart drop when the doors close. He's gone through similar bouts with the stroke stuff before, but never anything this serious. In fact, the last time they thought he had a stroke, they weren't one hundred percent sure, so they had to run a battery of tests on him before confirming that it was a stroke.

The bell dings and the silver door slides open. An oval nurse's station occupies the front of the floor, and there's no way of missing it. A heavy set woman, in her late 40's, is on the phone taking orders from a doctor as I catch her eye. Holding her finger up, she signals for me to wait.

Impatiently, I start craning my neck, trying to peer inside the rooms to see if I can find my dad himself, but most of them have curtains preventing anyone from seeing beyond the doorway.

"Can I help you?" she asks, replacing the phone back on its cradle.

"Yes, my dad, William Rogers, is here? I'm not sure what room he's in, but he had a massive stroke this morning and —,"

"What's your name, please?" she cuts me off. I can tell her patience with me is thin; she probably gets a million people a month rambling about their loved ones, and I'm no different.

"Mason Rogers," I say as she looks at the computer monitor.

"He's in room 302. Please be quiet upon entering, try not to disturb the patient, and if you need anything, we're right here."

I nod and glance around at the numbers posted

outside each door. Spotting 302, I slowly enter, afraid of what I might see. I'm so scared what he's going to look like, and honestly, I don't know if I can handle seeing him in much worse of a state than he already was at the nursing home.

"Dad?" I say quietly as I enter. He's hooked up to an IV and has a nasal cannula to help him breathe. It looks as though he's sleeping, and I'm afraid to wake him; she said not to bother him.

The monitors on the flash numbers and display his heart rhythm. His skin is ghostly white, and his white hair looks greasy and is standing on end. He looks so fragile, so weak. I've never seen him look this bad.

Taking a seat at his bedside, I place my hand on top of his and say a few words, willing him to get better. The slow lull of the monitors put me to sleep for, I don't know how long. An hour? Maybe two?

I'm woken up by the sound of a familiar voice. "Mason?"

My eyes flutter open, and I think I'm dreaming for a second when I look up and see Penny standing on the other side of his bed. I realize that it's not a dream as I notice she's wearing hospital scrubs with a stethoscope around her neck and a name tag.

"Penny?"

CHAPTER TWENTY-THREE

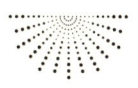

PENNY

My heart dropped when I saw Bill come in this morning as they admitted him to the ICU. I knew it would only be a matter of time before I'd be face to face with Mason again.

"Do you need anything?" I ask him as he stands on his feet. "A pillow? A blanket? Something to drink?"

"What are you doing here?" He asks, keeping his voice low as he glances down at his dad.

"I work here," I say. "I just started a few weeks ago."

"How is he? And don't give me a bullshit response. Tell me how he really is."

There's so much emotion and strain in his voice. He looks like he's on the verge of tears, and, honestly, so am I. I hate seeing his dad like this just as much as he does.

"The doctors said they don't know what his recovery

will look like. We won't know until he's more stabilized. Right now, they have him on some medications, and they're running tests." I look him over, and it's obvious that he came straight from work. "Are you okay?"

Running his hands through his hair, he says, "No, I'm not okay."

Checking the monitors, I chart his vitals and say, "I'm sorry, Mason. Let me know if you need anything."

He nods. "Thank you. I will."

An awkward moment of silence follows before I turn on my heels and make my way out of the room.

I know I've been wanting to see him, but not like this. I've got another six hours of my shift left before I can go home, and I don't know if I can make it through it.

When I came in this morning, I figured it'd be another day at work. Working in the ICU is never fun, but I like it because it makes me think and keeps me on my toes. It's crazy how fast someone's life can change at the drop of a hat.

"You can go out for break whenever you're ready," my co-worker Brandy says to me.

"Thanks. I just made rounds to check vitals," I pause. "Do you think you could take care of room 302 for today?"

"Why? Is something wrong?"

"No," I say. "Well, sort of. The man that's in there, his

son is here with him, and we have a past together. It's just that it was kind of awkward, and I don't know if it's such a good idea for me to go back in there."

She laughs and waves me off. "Penny, sometimes you have to do what needs to be done. You're caring for a patient; nothing more, nothing less. You'll be fine."

She's completely serious and isn't even entertaining the idea of giving me a break. "Okay," I sigh. "I'm going to head to the cafeteria. Do you want anything?"

Brandy shakes her head. "No, thanks."

I've never been so relieved to get on the elevator to go down for my break. Looking at myself in the stainless steel doors, I make an ill attempt to straighten my hair and tidy my makeup. There's nothing glamorous about my job, but it makes me feel good to help people.

Sitting at a small table near the window, I stare out at the busy street and watch the cars go by as I think about how terrible things must be for Mason right now. I didn't want to tell him that the doctor said his dad might not have a good outcome. Even though we haven't talked in a while, I wanted to give him some hope. Sometimes, having a little faith makes all the difference.

The small salad I picked up from the cafeteria tastes like shit, so I push it to the side and sip on my iced tea as I begin daydreaming what Mason's morning must've been like today. I can only imagine what went through his mind when he got the phone call.

"Hey," I feel a tap on my shoulder.

Turning around, I look up and see Mason standing behind me. "Hey," I say back to him.

"Mind if I have a seat?"

His eyes look hopeful, and I don't have it in me to tell him no. I wouldn't say no to him anyway, even if it does hurt me to see him because I still have feelings for him. I think Mason and I would've been a great couple, but I know he thinks otherwise. Scooting the chair out with my foot, I nod toward the seat across from me. "Be my guest."

Taking the empty seat, he half smiles at me. "Never thought I'd run into you this way," he says.

"I know, it sucks." I realize that my words might not have been the best choice. "I mean, I'm glad to see you, but it sucks that your dad is here."

Sipping his coffee, his eyebrows shoot up. "I know. I knew what you meant. So tell me, how bad is it? Really?"

"I already told you," I say to him. "And what your dad really needs right now is for you to be strong for him. When he comes to, he's going to need your support."

"You know, I feel really shitty. I feel like it's my fault for sticking him in that damn nursing home. Maybe if he wasn't—,"

"Mason," I stop him right there. "Listen to me, I know

you hated your dad being in there, but he was going to have this stroke regardless of the care he received. It wouldn't have mattered if he was at home in his own bed or if he was at the nursing facility. Sometimes we can't control what's going to happen, so you stop that nonsense right now."

He's quiet for a few minutes, sipping his coffee from the styrofoam cup, courtesy of the grotesque cafeteria. "I also feel like shit for what happened between us," he finally says.

Wow, did he just say what I think he's saying? Not wanting to assume anything, because I'd die of embarrassment if I read too much into his comment, I ask him what he means.

"Penny," he reaches across the table, grabbing my hand. "I'd be a liar if I said I didn't have feelings for you because I do. I care for you a lot."

"But?" I ask.

"But Lucas and I made a pact a long time ago." He lowers his voice so that we can't be overheard. "The reason why I said the things I did is because we both agreed that once we share a girl, neither of us can stake claim to her."

"But why, Mason? What's wrong with us liking each other and giving our relationship a real shot? It wouldn't be so bad."

"That's the thing, I want us to be together—as a couple, not a trio—but you've got to look at it where I'm coming from."

"Which is?" I press. I'm want to understand, I'm trying to understand, but it sounds like gibberish to me.

"Penny," he leans in closer to me. "You were fucking my best friend; my best friend and me. If you think Lucas doesn't like you, you're wrong. We both like you, so—,"

"He might like me, but we don't have the same type of relationship, Mason. For starters, Lucas has never spent any one-on-one time with me, we've never talked on the phone or texted, I've never met any of his family or anything like that. It's a completely different relationship."

He opens his mouth to speak, but I don't give him the opportunity.

"Mason, I love you, and I look at Lucas as more of an acquaintance. The way I feel about you is why I've stayed away this whole time. What we have is so much different, and even though you pushed me away, I still want to be with you."

Placing his hands on the back of his neck, he exhales a deep sigh. "But what about Lucas and I? Even if you only view him as an acquaintance, there's still the fact that we're best friends and we had a deal."

"You need to decide what you want, Mason. I can't

make your decisions for you, but what's Lucas going to say? Do you think he likes seeing you sad? And don't tell me that you aren't or that you weren't because he's the one who stopped by my apartment begging me to come to your house. He told me all about how you were practically moping around and said that it'd be good for me to come over."

"He did that?" he asks, stunned.

"Yeah, he did. And think about it, Mason, don't you think that Lucas wants to see you happy?"

My eyes are watering as I try to plead my case with him, but I'm not sure it's doing any good.

CHAPTER TWENTY-FOUR

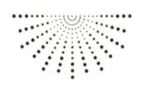

MASON

Listening to her talk, she makes a lot of sense. She's completely right. Lucas would never discourage me from being with someone that makes me happy, and if he did, that would mean that we weren't as good of friends as I thought we were.

I've never looked at it the way Penny has. The worst thing that would happen is that Lucas and I no longer share girls because I'd be in a committed relationship. It'd be no different from any other time I was seeing someone.

But it would also mean that I'd be breaking the pact, which is something neither of us has ever done. I know for a fact that there was one girl in particular that he liked, her name was Kerry. He'd hinted around that he wouldn't mind dating her, but it was me who reminded him of the pact. I don't want to go behind his back and do something that I may have prevented him from doing at one time. That would make me look like a shitty friend.

I'm still trying to process the fact that he was the one who went to Penny's apartment and talked to her when I was in a funk. It makes me wonder if maybe he knew all along how I felt about her. Neither of us has mentioned Penny's name since the night she left for good.

"I know Lucas wants to see me happy, but it puts me in such a bad place. You know? He's my best friend, and we've always shared girls. This was an agreement that we made a long time ago, and I don't want him to hate me for it."

She laughs. "He's not going to hate you for it, Mason. But if you want me back in your life, I think we need to decide what we're going to do because I don't want to be shared by the two of you. I only want you."

"Only me?" I ask. I heard her right, but I want to hear her repeat it.

"Only you," she squeezes my hand. "Mason, you're what I've wanted my entire life, but could never find."

I smile, "Right."

"Seriously," she says. "I've always wanted a guy who was a hard worker, someone who was fun, loyal, caring, and decent. You're all of those things and then some."

Hearing her say all of these things about me makes me

realize that it doesn't matter what anyone thinks. It also makes me realize how much I love her, too. I was scared to admit it—even to myself—but after hearing how she feels about me, straight from her own mouth, I know that we were meant to be together.

She's the one.

The only one.

"So, uh, how does this work? Am I supposed to ask you to be my girlfriend or something?" I tease, giving her a wink.

Grinning, her eyes light up. "Well, that'd be a nice start. Don't you think? And, oh, I don't know, maybe you could take me out to dinner, maybe a nice restaurant?"

It occurs to me we've never done any sort of date before.

"Holy shit, I've never taken you out before, have I?"

"Nope," she shakes her head. "Not unless you count the nursing home trips as dates, but I don't think those are very romantic."

Her face scrunches up, and her nose crinkles. She looks adorable. "Tell you what, as soon as my dad's out of here, I'll buy you the best steak in all of St. Louis."

"Deal," she says, checking her watch. "I better get back upstairs. My break was over five minutes ago."

"Here, I'll walk with you," I say, grabbing my coffee.

"I'm probably going to stick around for a while, at least until my dad wakes up, and then we'll play it by ear."

Almost two days later, my dad finally comes to in his hospital bed. His speech is very slurred and he's even more agitated than usual.

"S-s-son," he stutters. "W-where am I? Am I?"

His language doesn't make complete sense, and I feel awful for him. "It's okay, dad. You're at the hospital. You had a stroke. How are you feeling?" I ask as I press the button for his nurse to come in. I wish Penny were here to see him when he woke up.

"Is everything okay?" the nurse walks in.

"He's awake," I say. "He seems a little confused."

She nods and grimaces, "It's common for a lot of stroke patients. I'll call his doctor in to come examine him."

"W-where is she?" he asks.

"The nurse? She went to get your doctor dad. Relax, it'll be okay," I smile, giving him a reassuring nod.

"No," he tries to sit up, but he can't because he's too weak. "P-p-p-pretty P-p-penny, my girl."

How in the world he's still asking about her all these

months later and after waking up from a stroke is beyond me. "You'll see her soon, dad. I promise."

"Me, I mean, I-I heard her," he says.

"You did? When?" He's not wrong, he could have heard her voice many times, but I can't believe he'd remember it since it was unconscious.

Instead of answering me, he drifts back to sleep until the doctor comes in and rouses him.

"William?" the doctor says as he pulls back the covers on my dad. "How are you doing today?"

My dad opens his eyes and stares at the doctor; it's clear he doesn't know who he is. "My n-name's Bill."

"Bill, can you tell me where you're at?"

He looks around the room and stares at the window. "H-h-home."

"No, Bill, you're not at home. You're at the hospital. You had a pretty big stroke. Do you know what today is?"

My dad shakes his head no. He's completely out of it and doesn't know very much of what's going on. "No, go h-home," my dad mumbles.

"Well, you can't go home, Bill. But if you recover quickly, we can send you back to your room at the nursing home and you'll be good as new in no time. Can you look at the light?" The doctor asks, checking dad's eyes with a tiny light scope.

"No!" dad says, spit pulling in the corner of his mouth. "I g-go home."

It kills me to know that he remembers home and wants to be there, but I can't take him on. There's no way I could ever work, and Lucas needs me to help finish this job and run the business. We're a team.

After the doctor finishes examining dad, the nurse brings him a tray in hopes that he'll eat. "He needs to get his strength up," she explains. "Try to get him to eat a couple of items off his tray, or at least drink the broth. If you need anything, just let me know."

I send Penny a quick text to let her know that he's awake as I try to get him to eat something, but he's refusing everything. He doesn't want to eat, drink, or talk. I've never seen him this bitter, not even when he initially went into the nursing home.

Penny shoots me a text back saying that she's coming to the hospital. I text her back to let her know that she doesn't have to come since it's her day off, but she insists. She's such a good girl. I don't know how I got so lucky when I found her, but I'm glad that I did.

A half an hour later, Penny struts into my dad's room like she owns the place. She looks incredible wearing a white floral dress with her hair flowing around her shoulders.

"Hey, Bill," she says as she approaches his bed. "I came to see you!"

Dad opens his eyes and looks right at her, then smiles. Using his good hand, he puts his hand on hers. "My p-pretty P-p-penny. I m-m-missed you."

Smiling down at him, she pats his hand. "I've missed you, too." Turning to me, she asks, "What did the doctor say when he was in here?"

"Let's go out in the hall," I say.

Following me out to the hall, I tell her how dad didn't know anything and stared out the window. "That's okay," she says. "It's common. I know I'm not an expert, but I've been here for a little while now, and a lot of these people don't know what happened to them or why they're here when they first wake up."

"I feel so bad for him, Penny. He kept insisting on going home. There's no way I can take him in, and I know he doesn't want to go back to the nursing place."

"What if he didn't have to?" she asks.

"No, he has to, because what else am I going to do with him? I can't quit my job."

"Maybe we can work something out," she suggest.

"Like what?"

"What if I helped? If you quit working construction with Lucas and found work to do during the evenings, we could take turns."

"How, Penny? You work and go to school, and I can't just quit my job with Lucas. We've already got enough to sort out as it is. He'll kill me if I say I'm not going to work with him either. He's counting on me."

"Mason, I think you need to give Lucas a little more credit, because I've already talked to him."

"You did what?"

CHAPTER TWENTY-FIVE

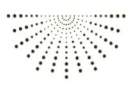

PENNY

Brandy called me as soon as Bill woke up and I knew that he wouldn't want to go back to the nursing home. He probably doesn't have much time left as it is because he's had so many strokes and each one gets progressively worse.

"I made a few phone calls," I say to Mason. "I talked to the ADON who runs the nursing program at my school, and we were able to work out part of my schedule so I can do some of my daytime classes in the evenings—at home, on the computer. I also called Lucas."

He runs his hands through his hair and wraps his fingers around his jaw. "This ought to be good. What did you say?"

"I told him about your dad and how I could help take care of him if you were to bring him home. We talked about your job, and how he might be able to wing it without you."

"Wing it without me? How the hell is he going to do that?"

"It's not easy," I say. "I called him last night after I got home, and he said that he has a friend of the family who lives by the job you guys are doing in Hayti. He said that the guy's out of work and has a baby on the way so he could use the extra cash. Lucas was going to see if the guy could take your place to finish out this job."

"And what am I supposed to do for money? I'm not taking a job working at a burger joint for minimum wage in the evenings," he says, defensive.

"No, not at all. You're good at construction, right? What if you opened your own business and became your own boss?"

He twists his fingers through his hair in frustration. "What are you saying? I don't know where you're going with this," he groans.

"Your house is in dire need of repairs and updates, right? Take some time off work, fix up the house; make it more suitable for us. Your dad can have the second bedroom, so work on that first. While you're renovating your house, we'll figure something out. Anyone can start a business these days. Maybe you could get a small business loan and open your own construction company. You could do bids in the evenings when I'm at home with your dad, and check up on the job sites after I get home from work or school."

"That's a lot to ask, Penny. I don't know about it."

Looking him dead in the eye, I say something that I know will resonate with him, something he'll understand. "I do know one thing, Mason. If you send your dad back to that nursing home, you're going to cut what little time he has in half. If you want to keep him around as long as possible, you'll bring him home, and we'll take care of him together. We'll find a way to make it work."

My words ring all too true to him because I can see it in his eyes. He knows what I'm saying is true. "Let me make sure that Lucas can get that guy to cover for me down in Hayti. Okay? I have to talk to him before I do anything."

"Okay, but you'll see. Let's go back in there with your dad."

The two of us pull up a chair next to his dad's bedside and pretend to watch the tiny television in the room. I couldn't be less interested in what's on TV because the last couple of days have been a whirlwind for me; an emotional roller coaster.

"Wait a minute," Mason says, keeping his voice low, so he doesn't wake his dad. "How'd you get Lucas's phone number? I thought you said that you two never talked or texted?"

I smile. "There's this thing called Google, and I know the name of his construction company, so I looked up the number."

He nods and laughs, "Oh, yeah, I guess you're right." A few more seconds of silence pass. "Wait, if you talked to him, does he know that we're a....couple?"

"Mhm," I nod. "And he's perfectly fine with it. He was happy for us, actually. You're not exactly stealthy when it comes to hiding your feelings, Mason. I think we all knew from the get-go that you and I were going to end up together; otherwise, why would Lucas have come to my apartment to invite me to your house that night it snowed? He knew how much you missed me, and I think you knew it, too."

A loud sigh escapes his lips. "So, you and him both knew the whole time? How much I liked you? And that I was falling in love with you?"

I nod, "Yep, I think we were waiting on you to make the decision for yourself."

"You two are a bunch of fuckers, you know that?" he bursts into laughter.

"Yeah, but we're two fuckers who love you and always look out for you."

Bringing his dad home was the best thing we could have ever done. He's doing much better than he was in the nursing home, and it wasn't for lack of care. The place where he was treated him well, but it's his will to live. He wants to thrive, and he's doing just that from the comfort of his own home.

"P-penny," he says, "when is my s-son coming home? I want t-to talk to him."

"He'll be home after he runs to the bank. Do you need anything, or is there something I can do?" I ask.

He motions his finger for me to come closer, so, of course, I oblige. "I w-want grandkids."

My eyes about fall out of my head, and I have to close my mouth. "Yeah, I think you're going to have to talk to Mason about that. It might be a while before we get to that point."

His dad smiles at me and lies back in the bed, so I let him rest while I tidy up the house. Mason's really taken what I said to heart and started remodeling parts of the house. He did his dad's room first, of course, and now he's working on the kitchen, which needed an update like yesterday.

He started with ripping out all of the cabinets, which created a ton of dust, and a lot of mess. Dishes have been piled up all over the kitchen for almost two weeks now, but the new cabinets will be delivered by this weekend. I tried to get him to wait, but he wanted to repaint the kitchen before he installed the new cabinets, and the new countertop will go in as soon as he gets everything else finished. Once he does the cabinets and counter, he'll start tearing up the kitchen floor, and I can't wait for that.

"Hey, babe," he says, walking in with a manila folder, grinning like a goon.

"What's that?" I ask.

"This? It's our future, babe. I did a lot of thinking about what you told me, and I decided something."

"Tell me more," I say, smiling along with him. Whatever he's got in mind has to be good, and I'll support him one hundred percent in whatever he does.

"I've really enjoyed remodeling our house. It's nice to see this old, run down house turn into something beautiful."

"With my help!" I butt in.

"Yes, with your help," he kisses me on top of the head. "So, I've decided to do what you told me to do: open my own business."

"Doing what? Remodeling houses?" I ask.

"Better," his grin spreads ear to ear. "Flipping houses. When you're at school or work during the day, dad and I sit around watching TV. There was a show on about flipping houses, and I thought I could do it, too."

"How does that work?" I ask.

"We buy a house on the cheap, I get the supplies on a loan, do the work myself—minus electrical because I hate electrical work—and then sell it for profit."

I frown, "And how are we going to pay for all of this? What if the house doesn't sell? Then what?"

"It'll be fine, babe. I've done my homework. Sometimes, I think about things and research them before I bring them up to you, and I put a lot of research into this." I roll my eyes because I don't see how any of this could be profitable. A lot of the houses in the area are only selling for fifty-thousand or less, sometimes only half of that. "Listen, babe, you know how a lot of the houses are selling really cheap around here? Well, do you know that a similar house in a similar neighborhood is selling for over two-hundred grand?"

"Yeah, but how much time and money are they putting into those houses?"

"It doesn't matter," he says. "Even if it takes me eight to ten months to redo one house, and it sells, I'll have made a hundred and fifty grand profit. In one year, on one house. If I can get some helpers and do two a year, that's over three hundred grand a year, babe. Over a quarter mill per year!"

His idea sounds fantastic, I just hope he can make it work.

"Oh, hey, your dad wants to talk to you, by the way."

"About what?" he says, taking a bottle of water from the fridge.

"Um, he wants us to start having kids."

Water sprays from his mouth all over the kitchen. "He what?"

I laugh and point toward his room. "Yeah, you might want to go set him straight on that."

EPILOGUE

I knew I was onto something with flipping houses. I've made enough money in the last few years that Penny doesn't have to work, but she wants to. She said she didn't go to school to sit at home and do nothing. I can't blame her, I'd go nuts if I sat at home all day long.

We had a small courthouse wedding about a year after we started living together, and just like her old apartment, Penny hung our pictures up all over the house. My favorite is the one of her showing off her wedding ring. She's standing beside me, holding the back of her hand toward the camera, pointing to her ring. I can't help but smile every time I walk past that picture.

Dad passed away a few days ago, and even though he's no longer with us, I'm grateful for the time that he spent in our home. I wouldn't have been able to do it without

Penny. She's changed my life in so many ways, and I don't know what I'd do without her.

"Babe? Can you take Olivia while I get dressed? Make sure she doesn't crawl on the floor and get her dress dirty. I want her to look nice at your dad's wake."

Olivia just turned eleven months old. It makes me sad that her grandpa won't get to watch her grow up, but at least he got to meet her and spend his final days with her. I'll never forget the first time he saw her.

His mind started to rapidly deteriorate during Penny's pregnancy. Some days were good, some were bad, but as soon as we brought Olivia home from the hospital, his eyes lit up, and he knew exactly who she was.

He laid in his bed with his arms completely outstretched, eager to hold her. I was so scared to let him take her, but Penny assured me that it would be okay, and it was. He looked so proud, and I was happy to give him a grandchild.

Taking Olivia out of Penny's arms, I take her into the living room and call Lucas.

"Hey, I'm on my way," he answers the phone.

"No problem, I was just calling to make sure. Thanks for being one of the pallbearers for my dad," I say.

"I wouldn't miss it for the world. I'll meet you at the funeral home."

I play a game of peek-a-boo with Olivia while we wait

for Penny to get ready. It doesn't take her long to come out fully dressed, and she looks stunning.

"You look gorgeous, babe."

"Thanks," she says. "Can you tell I've been crying? I put on my waterproof mascara, but I started crying while I was putting it on."

Burying her head in my chest, she begins sobbing. She and my dad grew so close, and she's taking it harder than I expected.

"Hey," I tilt her face toward mine. "Nobody cares if you've been crying. It's to be expected. I know dad wouldn't mind," I try to make her laugh.

She cracks a grin, which is close enough, and takes Olivia from me. "Come on, we should get going so we can greet the rest of the family."

Lucas gets to the funeral home just minutes after us. While I'm busy talking to the funeral director, Lucas walks in, and Penny leaves my side to go greet him. I watch them hug and then kiss each other on the cheek, but there's no jealousy because I know she's all mine.

Leaving the front office, I step into the hallway to join Penny and Lucas, and I see a woman standing next to him.

"Hey, brother," he hugs me. "How are you holding up?"

I shrug, "Good, I guess." I nod toward the woman, "Who's this?"

Lucas smiles at me and puts his hand against the small of her back. "Mason, this is my girlfriend, Nikki."

"Hi, Nikki, it's nice to meet you."

"Likewise," she shakes my hand. "Lucas has told me so much about you. He said you two are best friends, and just introduced me to your gorgeous wife."

I smile at Penny, "Yes, that would be her. Our pretty Penny."

A tear rolls down Penny's cheek as I call her by the nickname my dad called her. Nikki looks at Penny and smiles.

"You should try not to get so upset in your condition," Nikki says, pointing to Penny's stomach.

I can't believe that she's insinuating that Penny's fat enough to look pregnant. She's practically the same size she was before she ever had Olivia. Glancing over at Penny, I try to gauge her reaction because with the emotional roller coaster she's been on, she's liable to punch this girl right in the face.

Penny's jaw is hanging open as she stares at Nikki. "Why would you say that?" She asks her.

"Because you're pregnant," Nikki says, rubbing Penny's stomach as she grins. "It's so obvious."

Penny pulls away from her and wraps her arms

around her waist. Tucking Penny against my side, I say, "Come on, babe. We've got other stuff to do," and walk her away from Lucas and his girlfriend as he asks her what her problem is.

We're almost to the viewing room when Penny stops and looks up at me. "She's not wrong, Mason."

"Don't be ridiculous. You don't look pregnant; that woman's just a bitch. You look wonderful."

"No, I am pregnant, Mason."

"What?" I ask. I can't believe my own ears. How would I not know if my wife was pregnant?

"I was waiting until your dad started feeling better before I announced it to the family, but he never got better. Instead, he took a turn for the worse, and I didn't know how or when to tell you."

"Penny," I say, pulling her into my arms. "You should've told me right away. Any time is a good time. Are you okay? How far along are you? How did that lady know?"

She smiles up at me. "Women just have a way of knowing, I guess. I'm about two and a half months along."

"What? How long have you known?"

"A few weeks; I was definitely going to tell you before my first doctor appointment."

"When is that?"

"Monday?" she laughs.

"Penny Rogers, if you weren't pregnant, I'd spank your little round ass."

"I love you, Mason."

"I love you, too. Now let's go make sure dad's all situated so we can say our goodbyes."

Walking toward his casket, Penny whispers, "He knew, Mason."

I look at her, horrified. "He knew he was dying? I thought he was on all those meds so he would be out of it?"

"No, he knew that I was pregnant, and he was so happy, Mason."

A tear wells up in my eye as I think about how excited he must've been. "But how did you tell him? He was barely awake."

"Before most people die, they have a moment of clarity, where they're alert and alive. I knew it was coming, that it was the end, and I wanted him to know before he left us."

"What did he say?" I ask. God, I wish I could've been there for it, but I understand why she kept it to herself. She knew. She always knows everything. I don't know how, but she does.

"He was sitting up in bed, I was feeding him Jello, and he was so with it, you know?" I nod. "So, I told him that I had big news, that we were having another baby. He promised he wouldn't tell anyone—and he didn't, until he saw Olivia. He was gloating, Mason. Your dad was telling her how she would be a big sister, and that she'd have to look after her little brother or sister, and that she'd be my big helper."

I feel like I'm about to lose it. I've never heard anything more precious than the words she's speaking right now. Wiping a tear from my cheek, I try to compose myself before anyone sees me.

"I'm sorry, babe. I didn't mean to make you cry," she says. "I just wanted you to know that he knew, before we buried him. I want you to remember how happy he was when he was alive, and he was so happy that day."

God, I love this woman.

"Don't ever leave me, okay?" I make her promise.

"I won't ever leave you, Mason."

Clasping our hands together, we approach dad for one last time. It's then that I know this is how it was always supposed to be, and I couldn't have had a happier ending than this.

A NOTE FROM VIVIAN ABOUT "ONLY YOU"

Derek and I hope you enjoyed this story. The two of us sat down together one day—okay, several days—and brainstormed this novel for you. Yes, it was a quick read, but I swear to you, this book is novel length.

This is my first co-written book, and I couldn't be happier with how it turned out. I never thought I'd co-write with another author, but Derek's a pretty cool guy to work with and he listens to everything I tell him. Okay, most of the time he listens.

We wrote this story in about two and a half weeks, taking turns writing each chapter. Derek was Mason's (stubborn) voice, and I was Penny's voice. The hardest part was editing, of course, but it wasn't too bad. We tried to tighten it up anywhere possible, which is why this was

A NOTE FROM VIVIAN ABOUT "ONLY YOU"

such a quick read. I hate books that sag in the middle or slowly drag out the story forever and ever.

I've been asked a few times whether or not I'd write another book with Derek, and that answer is: absolutely! We wrote in Google docs, passing it back and forth, reading over what the other wrote, and responding to the previous chapter in our own voice. Sometimes, he'd change what I wrote and vice versa, but I think it made a better story.

Thank you so much for all of your support. A lot of you helped share teasers and spread hype about the book, and we are so grateful for your help. We each have some amazing readers and we couldn't do this without you. This book is FOR you.

If you're reading our work for the first time, come join us in our private reading group (Vivian's Voyeurs and Derek's Dirty Subs) where we both host a bunch of giveaways and have parties. I'm always giving away shit, and I like to scatter it about so it kind of loots the internet. Sometimes I hold giveaways in my group, on my fan page, on my website, and in random reading groups on Facebook.

Giveaways are always rampant around release time, because I love giving stuff away. You can stay up to date about our upcoming releases by following our newsletter so you know when and where to look.

A NOTE FROM VIVIAN ABOUT "ONLY YOU"

If you want to know more about us, you'll have to become a stalker. Derek is very elusive and mysterious, but he's also funny as hell.

I have family in Kansas City, Missouri, and my cousin introduced us over the summer when I went to visit family before the kids started school for the 2017 school year. Derek had always said that he wanted to be a writer, but he didn't know where or how to start.

My wonderful cousin (yes, that's with a pinch of sarcasm and a dash of love) said, "Hey, you should meet my cousin, Vivian. She writes and publishes her own books."

So, when I went to visit, Derek was hanging out in the backyard with the family, eating BBQ (hey, it's what we do in KC). I didn't think anything about it, just figured he was there as a friend of someone's.

That's when my cousin introduced us and we started talking about books. This is normal conversation for me because all I talk about is books (ask Jillian Quinn), so I didn't think anything of it. That's when Derek started asking questions about how to publish. I told him if he was serious, I'd help him.

I have so many friends and acquaintances who say, "Oh, you just sit and make up stories all day. It can't be that hard. I want to do it, too. Tell me what to do."

Once I start explaining the whole process (and it

really is a process), they slowly back away. They're like, "Oh, wait....there's work involved in this? I don't have time for that!" I didn't think Derek would stick around to learn it all, but he did and I'm happy for him because he has quite a bit of talent.

As for me, when I'm not busy "not working," you can find me scrubbing down my house, plotting my next book, writing, reading my Kindle, talking on the phone with Jillian Quinn, or chasing after my minions who aren't so 'minion' anymore now that they're all in school.

My advice to anyone who wants to write is do it! Seriously, plot the story, or pants it, whatever, and write it. You can always edit it later. Never, and I mean never, ask friends or family to read your work to see what they think. You're never going to tell someone they stink (even if they do), so your family's not going to say anything critical about your work.

You can post snippets of it online to get real critique, and don't think you're horrible if you see some unkind remarks. When someone dings me in a review, I pay attention to that review because there is always room for improvement in anything we do. Writing is a craft that can never be truly mastered because the market is always evolving and changing, and the trends and tropes can change overnight.

Above all, the most important thing you can do is

A NOTE FROM VIVIAN ABOUT "ONLY YOU"

read. Read. Read. Read. Read, and read some more. You can study what works and what doesn't, what you do and don't like, and so on. I never see another author as competition—even the big ones—I see them as milestones. Like I said, there's always room for improvement.

On that note, I've rambled enough. Happy reading!

DEREK'S DARK DESIRES

Subscribe to my Dark Desires newsletter and get a FREE copy of Riot instantly! Riot is a full-length novel that is only available to subscribers!

Once you have your free book, you will have the advantage of knowing when I will be releasing my next title, when I'm having special deals, and you'll be the first to know the next time I have some cool stuff to give away (you can unsubscribe at any time).

CLICK HERE TO SUBSCRIBE NOW

VIVIAN WARD NEWSLETTER

Get free books, ARC opportunities, giveaways, and special offers when you sign up for Vivian's newsletter. We all get enough spam so your information will never be shared, sold or redistributed in any way. You'll instantly receive a free novel just for signing up that isn't available anywhere else!

newsletter.authorvivianward.com

ABOUT THE AUTHOR

Derek Masters is an erotic romance author from the Kansas City, MO area. He graduated from the University of Kansas with a degree in criminal justice, but discovered that writing was his true passion. You can often find him talking sports at local hole in the wall bars or working on his next novel in a crowded coffee shop.

www.derekmasters.com
derek@derekmasters.com

ALSO BY VIVIAN WARD

Please check out my website for a complete list of all of my novels. If you enjoyed the book you just read, please consider taking a moment to let me know by leaving a review on Amazon and/or Goodreads. I appreciate your support more than I could ever express!

www.authorvivianward.com

Made in the USA
Columbia, SC
16 February 2018